Crossing the River

An Anthology in Honor of Sacred Journeys

Edited by Literata Hurley

Copyright © 2014 by Neos Alexandrina

All rights reserved. No part of this book may be reproduced by any means or in any form whatsoever without written permission from the author(s), except for brief quotations embodied in literary articles or reviews. Copyright reverts to original authors after publication.

Table of Contents

Introduction
    by Literata Hurley   1

A Note From the EiC
    by Rebecca Buchanan   4

The Shaman and the Goddess
    by Joseph Murphy   5

The Song
    by Szmeralda Shanel   7

Con Rio
    by Karla Linn Merrifield   27

All the Colors of the Rainbow
    by Gerri Leen   28

Homecoming
    by Karla Linn Merrifield   45

The Seasons March
    by Kit Koinis   47

Mt. Kailash
    by George H. Northrup   52

Bargain with the Mountain King
    by Juli D. Revezzo   54

Some Kind of Orpheus
    by Valentina Cano   80

Into the Light
    by Ruth Sabath Rosenthal   81

Space Journey
    by Kristen Camitta Zimet   83

Myself to Myself
    by Scathe meic Beorh   85

I shall set free my hair and wear a fawn skin
    by Rebecca Lynn Scott   92

Passing Through the Portal
    by Elizabeth Bodien   100

Walking the Labyrinth
    by Kristin Camitta Zimet   102

She Who Holds the Reins
    by Brenda Kyria Skotas   107

Persephone
    by Valentina Cano   110

Walking Two Worlds
    by Larisa Hunter   111

Baptism in Four Reflections
    by Craig W. Steele   120

Nine Lives -- A Feline Cosmogony
    by Literata Hurley   123

The Shaman Visits the House of Dust
    by Joseph Murphy   128

Theseus, Considering the Ball of Thread
    by Hillary Lyon   132

Orion: An EcoFable
    by Rebecca Buchanan   134

Hadrian in Hyperborea:
The Enigma of the Emperor's Wanderings
    by P. Sufenas Virius Lupus   137

Navigatio Gaii Suetonii
Paullini ex Britannia ad Ogygia et Insulas Saturni
    by P. Sufenas Virius Lupus   155

Our Contributors   170

About Bibliotheca Alexandrina   178

Current Titles   179

Forthcoming Titles   182

Introduction

In the Pagan world, metaphors having to do with journeys are very common. We speak of our "paths," which we discover and follow, which may converge and diverge, and which take us to unexpected places. As with so many ideas, we extend this metaphor to see where it may lead. This volume is a collection of works exploring the idea of journeys, especially the kind of journey that changes the person who undertakes it.

Most forms of Paganism are more present-oriented, and somewhat less teleological, than the prevalent forms of Christianity; this may contribute to a tendency for Pagans to focus on the journey rather than the destination. Wiccan metaphors, in particular, tend to draw on spatial ideas of circles and spirals rather than a straight path towards a defined conclusion. Combined with structural factors that make Paganism often an individualized pursuit, much of this discussion of paths and journeys concentrates on constructing a coherent narrative of one's own history and situation. The desire for coherence in this self-explanation encourages people to emphasize what is connected and continuous about their metaphorical path. Looking at the ways this metaphor is used as a description of smooth, gradual processes made me want to examine the differences: what breaks up a journey? What about the boundaries that change us as we cross them?

When a journey is a metaphor for the passage of time, it is clear that critical boundaries include birth and death. The title *Crossing the River* was chosen in part as an allusion to the ancient Greek myth of the river Lethe as a defining boundary in the underworld, which reminds us of the ways that water defined the geography of less technological world when crossing a river as part of a physical journey was a major undertaking and a very real danger.

This association of water with risks and the unknown leads to imagery of death and rebirth, which had ritual significance even before Christianity adapted a specific ritual washing for baptism. But the kind of death and rebirth that are possible through water are very different experiences than that of, say, the phoenix, with its fiery metaphors. Water is also associated with the unconscious, which is with us always. The phoenix's transformation is comparatively easy, because it is completed in a few seconds, and a simple immolation of the old leads to total renewal. Water, by contrast, draws us into itself for an extended period, forces us to examine the dark, unknown, and potentially suffocating depths, and come to terms with what is inside us before we emerge changed.

Myths, storytelling, and poetry are some of the most important ways that we shape our metaphors. The works in this anthology come from a variety of perspectives and use diverse approaches to the concept of journeys. What I looked for in all of them was some expression of a sense of change, an idea that the self who journeys is transformed in the process, sometimes irrevocably so. Perhaps you, the reader, will find yourself changed, too.

Literata Hurley

November 2013
Arlington, VA

A Note From the EiC

Rebecca Buchanan

Journeys are strange things. It is their inherent liminality, I suppose. A journey is movement, crossing, betweenness. There is always a start and sometimes an end, but these are separate and distinct unto themselves. The journey itself -- and that is often *journeys*, simultaneous or overlapping, for one cannot move physically without also moving mentally and emotionally and spiritually -- is alteration, displacement, passage, progression; it is not static; it is the antithesis of static. And in this nonstatic state of betweenness there is change, evolution, transformation.

To be alive is to move. To live is to change.

Life is not a single journey, but a progression of journeys.

Time to get your feet wet.

The Shaman and the Goddess
Joseph Murphy

Spirits burst from the skin of my drum;
Nuzzled eye-sized stones
Illuminating my keel; neighing,
Eat the grain I offered.

Harnessed to my bow's beak,
They drew me toward the House of Night:
Through black water's claw-backed tides,
Past an undertow's bloodied mouth;
Into the calm of star-cloak and mist.

I moored to the sky's navel; the paths
Of day and night converged.

The gate opened as I spoke my true name,
First uttered by fire-souls
Who keep my drum's skin taut.

I entered the House of Day as the Goddess descended.

Here is what to remember, she said: "What is
Can only be, regardless of breadth
Or gleam; breath or rot.

"What is may seem less so, whether whole,
Torn, culled; well-carved
Or half-thought-out.

"*What is not is unknowable.* Engrave this
On your craft's mast; *to be* on your prow.
No mortal can then dissuade you
When you return."

With this, the gate reopened; I descended,
Setting aside my feather-bright mask.

The Song

Szmeralda Shanel

She awoke for the third morning with the last notes of the strange, nearly familiar, song in her head. In the past days the notes of the song had moved through her, danced around her, hung above her head like soft smoke. She kept catching small glimpses and pieces of the whole song, but the pieces were too small to hold onto or to pocket. The song was a fractured fragment, a thin slice of a memory that she couldn't quite remember and, because she couldn't remember it, she couldn't sing it. She could not sing it. Though the song crept around in her dreams every night, by day it would not be remembered. It held her closely as she slept, then left her sighing and longing each morning when she awoke, the last notes fading as her eyes opened.

"What is this song? Where does this music come from?" She lay in her bed, her soul trying to savor its sweet wild flavor. To hold it. To keep it. To know it. She knew that if she did not find it, the longing would drive her mad, so on the ninth night she asked for a sacred dream to give her a clue. That night she dreamt of a lighthouse that sparkled and tink-tinked with the song like a child's music box. There were drums too, a tambourine and a trumpet. And women were singing.

When she awoke the next morning she knew she had to find the lighthouse that held the music. "I will build a canoe and I will find my song." So she got an ax and she went to the woods, then she called out to the trees, "Is there anyone here that is willing to help me find my song? Is there any one of you who will be my canoe?" No tree responded, so she turned around and went back home. That night she lay in bed and wondered how she would make a canoe without wood. She fell asleep with trees on her mind.

That night in the woods, the trees spoke amongst themselves. "So, nobody's going to help that poor child find her song?" an old oak asked.

"Why you say it like that? All accusatory and what not, I don't see you volunteering yourself for the job," another tree responded.

"Hey, I'd be all about it if she didn't come up in here with that ax, I mean she was steppin' up like she was gonna just chop one of us down whether we volunteered or not. I don't like that, a damn ax, who does she think she is?" the old oak snapped.

"Well at least she asked, unlike those damn lumberjacks!" a maple tree called out.

"Oh yes! Those damn lumberjacks, can't stand 'em!" The trees all started to go off complaining about lumberjacks, people and their pissin' dogs and other such injustices that the rest of us never think about that trees have to endure.

"Well, I like her, that girl and I want her to find that music, or her song as she calls it. I think I'd like to go," the young tree said softly.

"Well now are you sure? I mean you're only 107 years old, not much more than a sapling, and once you're cut from your roots, well..."

"Yes, I'm sure. I will go with the girl."

The next morning the girl returned to the woods. This time she left her ax at home, instead she brought a gift for the trees. She sat down before them and sang a tree song, and when she was done she said, "I have sang for you your own special song. Is there any one of you that will help me find mine?"

The young tree fell to the ground, the girl thanked them all, then dragged the tree home with her. For many days she carved, painted, decorated and enchanted her canoe. When the moon was full she pushed it out into the ocean and hopped in.

She brought with her exactly what she thought she needed. Her Tarot deck, a quilt her sister made her. A journal, crayons, wine and water. A drum and a little stuffed green horse named Rogue.

She looked up at the sparkling darkness and cried out, "Mother above whose body is the starry heavens, look out for me, keep me safe."

She cast her eyes down to the shimmering darkness and whispered "Mother below, do carry me gently."

Then she sat back embraced by her quilt, journal in lap, crayon in hand, she drifted, sketching the shifting world around her, sippin' on warm wine. And she sang. She sang sea songs and rain songs. Earth songs and stone songs. Sun, moon and star songs. Wind songs, flame songs. Nonsense songs, righteous songs. Tragic songs and magic songs. Love songs that made her weep, as well as ones that made her laugh. She sang worker songs, dreamer songs, haunting songs and sleeping songs, and fierce rebel songs that made her raise her fist high and shout.

From night to day and day to night and night to day again. And she had fun, too. When she got hungry she ate whatever the sea provided and she never got sick or cold or lonely and when she got tired she would sleep.

Things went on this way until one evening when everything changed. The wind and the waves started moving wildly toward each other. The wind whipped at the ocean and the ocean waters jumped up and snatched at the wind. To the unknowing eye this would look like a fight, but really it was a dance. And the girl was caught in the middle of it. "Wind! Water! I don't know what you two are fighting about but for me in this little canoe it's very scary-- please stop." Poor little dear. Because the elements were not fighting they did not understand what she meant so they continued to joyfully twirl around together and the canoe flipped.

She struggled and fought and choked on the waves, terrified she would drown. "Squawk!" cried a seagull from above. "Sister, let go, stop thrashing about! Surrender to the waters and you may be saved!" it told her. So she took the gull's advice and released.

She spiraled down down down and down. And even further down. When her feet touched the ocean floor she continued to spiral down into the sand down down down and down. And then the spiraling stopped and she felt something soft and cushy beneath her feet. Grass. She could hear the crackle of little sticks. Around her all was dark, but in front of her was a bit of light. She took a few steps forward and came out of the opening in a tree trunk. As she stepped out an arrow flew past her left ear and something clunked to the ground. She turned to find lying behind and beneath her a huge beast. Before her stood a tall and handsome young woman with a bow in hand and quiver of arrows on her back.

"Humph. I see your demons dun tried to follow you here." The woman said, "Sorry if you wanted to keep 'em, but we got no room for your baggage. We better cook this up and make it useful." The woman grabbed the beast and effortlessly slung it over her shoulder.

"What is this place? Where am I?" the girl asked.

"You are right where you are at -- c'mon let's go," she was told.

"But who are you?"

"Hush now and c'mon fo' I leave your slow ass out here in deese woods and night falls."

The girl looked up into the sky, the sun was high and young. She thought to herself, "It can't be much later than early afternoon." But as soon as she had the thought this the sun in the sky dropped a bit and it was dusk. She decided she'd better follow the curious woman who was already steps ahead of her walking down the winding path in the woods. Somewhere off in the woods she heard whispering that she couldn't understand and giggles, too. "Who is that?" she asked the woman walking ahead of her at a pace she couldn't quite keep up with. But the woman didn't respond and she noticed as the sun continued moving downward bringing shadows with it that the young woman's figure seemed to transform in dramatically subtle ways. It seemed that her hips had filled out graciously and the bounce in her walk was replaced by a sway. She seemed shorter too. But the girl couldn't tell if this was really happening or if it was just the night settling in or her mind that had been scrambled from all of the spiraling inward and upward.

    A short walk and they had reached the woman's home. The sun was down, and the moon was up, a new thin sickle imprinted upon the sky. Inside a soft yellow light filled the room. There were herbs hanging from the ceiling and the air smelled of cedar and rosemary. The woman who was definitely old now removed the arrow and tossed the beast in a big black pot, filled it with water and things that the girl was unfamiliar with and started the water to boiling. When it was hot she sat the pot in the middle of the floor and gave the girl a long wooden straw.

    "Come now, and listen to me good. We learn from hard lessons and the discoveries we make in painful times are valuable and should be kept, but we do not need to carry old hurts and disappointments, anger, fear and resentments forever. Those burdens bend your back, and can continue to do so, so much that you'll wake up one morning to find that all you can feel is pain and all you can see is your own two feet."

"But I'm not angry."

"Um hum which is exactly why you were carryin' this thing around with you. Hush now and drink up. You'd be wise not to argue with me. You will go deep and when you come back you will know true strength. I will drum and you will dance. You'll keep what you need to remember and stay strong and you'll sweat out all the rest."

The girl was confused, but she did as she was told, she sipped that entire pot of water up her straw and when she got to the bottom of the pot no beast was found. Her skin hummed, it felt prickly, then sticky and warm. Suddenly she felt as if she had been struck by lightning, she was on fire and she screamed. The old woman began to drum and chant words foreign to the girl's ears. She danced and danced and revisited monsters she thought she had slain and fears that she had been unable to admit she was afraid of. She danced until all of these things filled the room, one by one she danced with them face to face and one by one they disappeared. When the drumming stopped the girl stood still but inside, the dance continued.

"Come now." The old woman said, and she took the girl into the bathroom and put her in the tub. The water was cold and smelled like roses. "Dip yourself 3 times 3 under then get out and dry off. That's nine times. And make sure you get out before you pull the drain else you go down with the water. You will sleep in the bed by the window. I'll leave something there for you to think on before you go to sleep." The old woman left. And the girl did as she was told, nine times under the water. Then she got out, pulled the drain and dried herself off.

She did not want to think on anything. She was exhausted and all she wanted to do was sleep. On her bed by the window she found a Tarot card: #17, the Star. She lay on the bed and studied the picture, she thought to herself how interesting it was that the old woman had the very same Tarot deck as she.

She was awakened the next morning by the sounds of singing, laughter and a sweet smell of sugar in the air. She sat up in bed and looked around. Where was the woman who had brought her here the night before? It didn't matter, the sugary smell was pulling her out the door already.

She followed the scent and that charming voice and came upon the most beautiful lady singing, dancing, and watering wild flowers. The woman wore a bright emerald green curly petticoat and a most impressive beaded halter top, gold and black like a bee. Her head was crowned with yellow sunflowers, and butterflies fluttered all about her. A jade colored snake with amber eyes coiled itself around and around the woman's waist. She was so beautiful that the girl, mesmerized, stood motionless watching her.

The woman stopped singing and smiled. "I know you are watching me. I should warn you that those who spy, who do not have the decency to introduce themselves, more than annoy me. In fact, those who watch me dance and listen to my songs without asking permission and then giving proper thanks are quickly transformed into beautiful swans whose necks I slit, whose feathers I pluck, and whose bodies I fry up and eat."

The girl wisely came out of her hiding and introduced herself. "I'm sorry to spy, I heard you singing and smelled your flowers, so."

"Oh you smelled my flowers? I do have a lovely garden. Tell me my dear, what kinds of flowers do you grow?" the beautiful woman asked.

"Oh me, I don't have a garden," the girl told her.

"Oh no my dear, *you* are the garden, but what kind of flowers do you grow? What is the beauty that you bring to the world?"

"Oh, well I've been told that I—"

"I have no interest in what you've been told." The beautiful one smiled.

"Okay, well, the beauty I bring to the world, well, I think..."

"No, not what you *think,* what you *know.* I'll ask you again to tell me, what is the beauty you bring to the world. Now take this, breathe deep, then sing it out." The beautiful woman handed the girl one of the sunflowers that crowned her head and repeated, "Breathe deep, then tell me."

The girl took the sunflower and held it up to her nose. She closed her eyes and inhaled deeply, then she exhaled and when she opened her eyes all of the colors around her were brighter, everything was luscious and luminous. She suddenly had the complete awareness of how alive the world around her really was. She smiled and watched everything breathing with her, the flowers, the trees, the sky above and the ground beneath. She lost her balance a bit, sat down and laughed. "I am wickedly humorous and richly romantic, beautiful. I understand the language of the stars, beautiful. I dream truths that have been and truths that will come, beautiful. I ride the back of the dragon topless dippin' in and out of rainbows, beautiful. When I laugh those around me feel my joy, beautiful. When I am angry I spit fire, it's beautiful but quite dangerous. The pots in my kitchen beg for my delicious concoctions, beautiful. Thread and wool in my hands tell a story, beautiful. I speak song and I can dance B-e-a-u-t-i-f-u-l!"

"Oh, you dance! Me too baby and dance we shall. Come on, we'll go to my house."

The two walked over a hill and came upon a yard filled with fruit trees, more wild flowers and a pumpkin patch. In the middle of it all stood the beautiful woman's home.

"Oh! A gypsy wagon, you live in a gypsy wagon?"

"The correct term, my dear, is *vardo*. And yes, I live here."

The vardo was gold, scarlet and indigo with hints of bluish green. It looked like a lusty sunset, with crystal stained glass of every shade of every color. Inside the sunlight streamed through that stained glass casting rainbow shapes and patterns all over the room. It was like being in a kaleidoscope. All along the walls were shelves that held tiny colored bottles. From the ceiling hung wind chimes and small brass bells. The woman put on a record and danced over to her tea kettle. She dropped in a handful of red flower petals.

"Tea kettles, flower petals, dreams and things seen and unseen. Taste and sip and drink my juice, laugh and dance and tell the truth." She poured two glasses of a thick red liquid, put one on her head, balanced the other on her knee, and did an impressive spin before placing them both on the table. "Gotta get it stirred up," she said, then sipped her drink. "We are queens!" The beautiful woman announced "Look at us sitting so lovely and regal in my glorious home -- oh I just adore myself! Don't you just adore yourself my dear?"

"Uhhh ... Sure." The girl mumbled. She smiled a small awkward smile and stared into her cup.

"Oh smile big! And drink up girl! There is so much joy and beauty in the world, but for some crazy reason, many simply refuse to see it. Why do you think that is?"

The girl sipped her flower drink, swished it around in her mouth, swallowed and raised her eyebrows "I suppose we are afraid to see it because we are afraid if we really see it we will love it too much and then there's always that awful chance and likelihood of eventually losing it."

"Oh? And tell me my dear, what have been your experiences with love?"

"Well now if you mean with the men folk, I'd have to say it's been a bit messy."

"A man, a woman, whatever. Love is love is love. What have been your experiences?"

The girl sipped more of her drink and thought back. "Well," she said, "I once had a guy who said he loved me, but love it was not. You know this guy, he wanted to jar me up the way a child does butterflies and lightning bugs in the summer time to study their wings and their glow. I stayed in that jar for a while too, but then I got my good sense back and remembered that no matter how many holes you poke into the top of the jar for air, if you don't let the little winged creatures out, they will eventually die. So I popped that top off and I left."

"I am glad to hear this, you know some young ladies never escape. They stay jarred up, caged in, bottled and boxed forever. Such a waste. You were smart to recognize that that was not love. He did not love you -- but what about you? Have you ever loved?"

"Love ... I'd have to say no. I've been in lust and I've been enchanted, but I can't say that I've ever really been in love. There was one who was very special and I almost could have loved him -- but I was afraid of a bleeding heart. Afraid of walking around with all of my soft spots exposed you know. He wanted me to trust him completely, to open up and all the rest. I tried hard too, and I finally did get to a place where I could take off all my armor, but my sword and shield I just couldn't put down; eventually he gave up and left. I miss him sometimes."

"That is a sad story indeed. I can see that you have some things to learn. I tell you what, I'll let you look into my magic mirror. Once you fall madly in love with yourself you will know better how to love others. Love is the greatest gift, and you should give what you want, take what you want and leave what you don't want, but only because you don't want it, not because you are afraid of it. Come here." The beautiful woman danced the girl over to the mirror and they looked in it together. The woman spun her around in circles, saying, "Gotta get it stirred up." She smiled at the girl, kissed her on both cheeks and left her alone in front of the mirror.

"This is such beautiful music you are playing. Who is the singer?" the girl asked.

"Why she's me of course! Who else would she be? Now stand there in front of this mirror quietly and concentrate, don't leave it until you have really seen yourself."

The beautiful woman crossed the room and sat on her bed. The girl turned back to face the mirror Her reflection stared back; at first she saw no difference in herself, she looked the same as usual. Then she noticed her skin glowing as if it had been dusted with gold, her black eyes shining with secrets. On her head sat a peacock feathered headdress and where there would be eyes in the tail feathers were sapphires, emeralds and obsidian. She felt eternal, radiant, beautiful and it was the first time she had ever really seen herself.

She laughed out loud and turned to thank the beautiful woman, but she was in bed and under the covers. The room was dark. The girl walked over to the woman's bed. Her crown of flowers were faded and wilting and the woman had lost her glow. She was sleeping and in her arms she had a little green stuffed horse. "Rogue," the girl whispered. But she didn't take it, she simply leaned down and kissed the beautiful one on the cheek, said thank you and left the vardo.

The sun was setting and the girl knew she should find her way back to the old/young woman's house that she had stayed in the night before, before it got dark. Too late the sun was down, the moon was up, and with the darkness came all kinds of strange voices. And with those strange voices, bright yellow eyes that peeked out from behind the trees. They giggled and whispered and called out to the girl asking her to join them. And the girl was curious, but she was more afraid, she was almost certain that the eyes and voices belonged to fairies and she had heard that fairies could be dangerous. So she just stood still and didn't respond to their calling.

They continued to sing out her name, giggling and calling her to them. She wanted to run, but which way to go? It was too dark to see anything but those eyes. Then she heard a trumpet and thought perhaps the beautiful woman who lived in the vardo was awake again. She decided to follow the trumpet back to the house. When she got to the trumpet she was not at the vardo. There in the middle of the woods stood a cool, mysterious, gorgeous dark woman in a long blue sequined dress that spread out like a fan at her feet. On her fingers silver jewelry, in her hand a silver trumpet, her hair thick, long and untameable.

"Don't be shy, come over here and sit down, child," the woman said. And so she sat down on a quilt spread out at the woman's feet.

"I heard voices whispering," the girl said.

"Yes, you did, Azzizas ... they are the forest spirits," the woman told her.

"Oh," the girl nodded.

"You have met my sisters?" the woman asked

"Yes, I think so, the beautiful woman who grows the flowers and the other two, the young one and the old one."

"The young/old one are just one, they are the same woman. My sister Adisa, she is a shapeshifter, she changes, transforms, dies, is reborn. Butterfly, snake, phoenix, that's her. She is very powerful and quite good at getting rid of what is no longer needed. And my other sister. She is joy and brings beauty wherever she goes. She travels through the dream landscape finding all the hidden beauty, then she brings it to light. She is wild passion and while she is beautiful, charming and much fun, it is best not to make her angry, she takes joy in all things and if you upset her she will take joy in destroying you. She goes as quickly as she comes you know but she doesn't die, she just sleeps. Sometimes she can be hard to wake up but it's important to remember when she's asleep, she's just asleep, not dead. Joy is like that always coming and going. Yes, you have met my sisters."

"And you?"

"Well, now I am the sister and the mother. The mystery that can only be encountered by the wise ones who dare to wander in the dark. Darkness is the oldest thing, the beginning and the end, wonderful and terrifying, nurturing one moment, devouring the next."

The woman stopped speaking and brought her trumpet to her lips and began to play. She swayed with her music, her hips rising and falling like waves on the ocean. The girl watched and listened and as she watched she noticed something like steam coming from the horn and the steam took shapes and the shapes told stories and answered questions to what seemed like some of the secrets of the world. The girl watched and listened and learned, she looked down at the quilt she was sitting on. It was her quilt of course and she smiled because this discovery did not surprise her.

The next morning she awoke on the forest floor feeling tight and slightly hung over. "There you are, girl, what are you doing sleeping out here on the ground?" a voice called. The girl looked up to find the familiar face of the young woman with the bow and arrows.

"C'mon, let's go." The girl followed her without any questions. She watched again as the sun fell from the sky and the woman shifted from young to old. Once inside she was told, "You have learned enough for now. Tomorrow you need to leave."

"I don't think I'm ready to go yet!" the girl cried.

"Well now that's just too bad because it's time for you to go," the old woman told her.

"But I'm still looking for something, I still haven't found my song."

"That's too bad. If you cared about it so much you wouldn't have lost it in the first place. Now go get in the tub and think about all that you've learned here so you won't lose that, too."

The girl did as she was told, but she was not happy at all. She was sure that if she stayed another day or two the song would come to her. It just wasn't fair that she had to leave already, just when things were starting to make sense. She started to cry just a little at first, but soon there were rivers of saltwater streaming from her eyes and down her cheeks. She cried so many tears that the tub began to fill up and overflow. Tears flowed and flowed. The girl suddenly noticed the mess she was making all over the bathroom floor and in a panic, before she remembered not to, she pulled the drain and the water rushed down, taking her with it.

Squeeze .... All is tight and black for a quick moment, then she is spiraling downward, water splashing in her ears and burning her nose. She suspects she may drown but then she feels something warm caressing her cheeks; she opens her eyes and sees the sun above her and the ocean all around her and in the distance, mixing in with the sounds of the waves and the whipping wind, she hears the song, in the distance she sees the lighthouse. She swims and when she gets to the shore she notices her canoe has made it there without her and inside are all of her belongings.

She runs right past it and up the stairs of the lighthouse. She can hear her song, voices singing it, drums and a trumpet. She gets to the top of the stairs and there is a door; she opens it to find the three women smiling at her, they are singing and dancing and waiting for her. She joins them, for the first time remembering the music and the words to her song. And they all sing together:

I am the earth air fire and water

the priestess the queen the mother the daughter

I am a daughter of sudden change

I am a daughter of storms and rain

when I twirl my skirt the winds stir gently

or they may blow rough tough and frightening

I am a daughter of honesty

a daughter of truth and inner searching

I look fear in the face strike it down with a "ha!"

I am a daughter of Oya

I am the earth air fire and water

the priestess the queen the mother the daughter

I am a daughter of life's beauty

of honey of joy and creativity

a daughter of vision, dance and sweetness

none can resist me I am their weakness

I am the spark that stirs your desire

the laughter you laugh

the flame in your fire

enchanting witch

inspiring muse

I am a daughter of Oshun

I am the earth air fire and water

the priestess the queen the mother the daughter

I am daughter of mysteries

I am a daughter of teaching dreams

a daughter of secrets and of silence

sometimes I'm calm

and sometimes I'm violent

wisdom and nurturance I hold

I am the push and I am the pull

Go to the ocean to greet my mama

I am a daughter of Yemaya

I am the earth air fire and water

the priestess the queen the mother the daughter

Con Río

Karla Linn Merrifield

I cruise aboard *M.V. Delphin II*
many miles on the *Rio Marañon*,
many miles on the *Rio Ucayali*,

downstream, upstream, downstream many miles before
the plotted course returns me again to the former *rio*.
Traveling thus many miles I cross *the* confluence.

I arrive at *the* equatorial epicenter
where *the* two tributaries converge.
I am where *the Rio Amazonas* is born.

Is it in crescent moonlight, or
in neotropical forest morning fog, or
in teaming rain that I am completely

swept away by *La Rio, via con Rio*, as silt
in the swirling country of countlessness?

All the Colors of the Rainbow
Gerri Leen

Anita sat in the small van, watching as it pulled into what had to be a tourist trap -- one of those restaurant/gift shops/open air bazaars that tour companies set up with the locals. She sighed, tired of being hit on. She'd opted for the van because the driver had promised her a tour of the "real Guatemala," not some tourist version that the big bus, now also sitting parked in the lot, had been offering.

If by real, the driver had meant a never-ending trip, then he'd delivered. The four-hour trip had already taken eight hours given his propensity to explore "interesting side roads" -- and the fact that he'd had to leave them by the side of the road when the military had commandeered the van. She and the Japanese family who were the only other passengers had conversed in rough Spanish -- the one language they shared -- about the odds of something worse than the military coming upon them as they waited for their driver.

The mother had thought the driver would abandon them; Anita had been inclined to agree with her. But he had come back, weaving down the road, honking, with his hand out the window waving furiously.

"Everyone ready to go?" he'd asked with a grin, as if standing around on the road halfway between Lake Atitlan and Guatemala City for twenty-five minutes had been their idea.

But as he regaled them with stories of the military, as he laughed and pointed out more interesting side roads, which mercifully he chose not to take, Anita let her bad mood go. This was Guatemala. She knew to expect the unexpected. It was magical if you let it be. It was maddening if you tried to control the experience.

He had pulled into the tourist trap an hour later, and while she was very glad to avail herself of the too-clean and shiny facilities -- definitely set up for tourists -- she was damned if she was going to buy more than a soda here.

She walked outside and roamed the market, not making eye contact with any of the vendors. The van was on its way to Chichicastenango and its famous market -- why in the world would she buy anything here?

When she worked her way to the end of the vendors and then back again, she saw a boy, probably about seventeen, with a blue and gold macaw sitting on a perch. The bird snapped at everyone that went by, but she walked up to it anyway -- it was less aggressive than many of the vendors here.

The bird studied her, head to one side, then to the other. Anita smiled at the kid tending it, looking for food that she could buy, but there wasn't any. The bird didn't seem to be for sale, nor was it there to earn money. It was just there.

She looked around, saw the Japanese family checking out the vendors. She turned back and talked to the bird. She'd always been this way, finding a stray dog or cat or whatever animal was handy to talk to rather than a human. Shy, her mother had said when she was little. Weird, her family said now.

Her boyfriend Jay had agreed, at the end, when weird no longer was quirky and charming, when he decided he'd rather be married to the girl in the cubicle next to him than to her. The girl who liked to ski and scuba and do all sorts of exciting things, who didn't live in her head instead of for real.

Anita wasn't exciting. In fact, if you looked in the dictionary under that word, she'd be listed as an antonym.

The bird dipped its head, and she took a chance and reached for it slowly. It shifted so its neck was within her reach, and she gently scratched, heard it make the happy sound she'd heard from the cockatoo in the pet shop back home.

"He likes you," the boy said with a smile. "He doesn't like anyone."

Of course he liked her. He was a damn bird, not a guy.

She held her hand out and the macaw stepped onto it. She continued scratching his neck with her free hand, saw her driver look over and shake his head and laugh. Then he motioned, pointing to the van.

She urged the bird back onto the perch, said goodbye to the kid, and took her place in the van, waiting as the driver rounded up her fellow travelers. She glanced over at the bird, couldn't see him or the boy. Then she saw the macaw, making its way across the parking lot, right toward the big tourist bus.

Her driver got in and the family scurried back to the van, talking in Japanese about something that made them laugh. They closed the door, and Anita saw the bird continuing its slow walk.

"Wait!" she said, and flung open the van door, moving faster than her mostly out-of-shape body liked to go, grabbing up the bird as it got way too close to the now pulling out bus and its huge tires. She heard a noise, looked up and saw that the people on her side of the bus were clapping.

The macaw just looked annoyed.

She took him back to the perch, saw the boy come running. "He never does that. He always stays here." The boy looked the kind of scared that said he loved the bird. "Thank you."

She gave the bird one last pat, then hurried back to the van.

"I'm going to add this to my list of colorful stories," the driver said, winking at her as she got back into the van and slid the door closed.

The Japanese family nodded, and the mother patted her awkwardly on the shoulder.

Their driver pulled out of the lot and began to whistle a tune she didn't recognize as he headed up the road to Chichicastenango.

***

The market in Chichicastenango was a kaleidoscope of color, each booth hung with weavings and masks, traditional Mayan designs and more modern representations of the art. Men and women walked down the narrow aisles, carrying samples, urging Anita to try their stall. They were less aggressive than the vendors at the tourist trap. They seemed to know by her eyes if what they carried interested her or not.

"Would you like to see how the huipiles are made?" a young woman asked her. She was dark and lithely beautiful in the Mayan way, with sharp cheekbones, almond eyes, and full lips under a cascade of shining black hair that hung down her back. "Come."

She took Anita's hand and tugged gently. Anita looked around, but no one seemed to be noticing them; there were none of the looks of concern she often saw on the faces of respectable merchants when a beggar or scammer came near their stores in the city.

Anita realized the woman had spoken English to her. "You aren't from here?"

"Oh, I am. I have travelled many places. Learned many languages. You look American, but you could be German, with that hair of sunshine." She ran her hand down Anita's blonde hair, cut into an easy bob. "So pretty." She met Anita's eyes. "My name is Shelly."

"Really? Shelly?"

"It's easier to say than my Mayan name." She grinned and Anita believed her -- Mayan names were not easy to wrap a gringo tongue around.

"I'm Anita." A name easy to say in so many languages.

"Well, Anita, I can give you a tour if you want?"

Ah, here was the scam.

"You get to see the real Chichi, and I get to practice my English."

Maybe not such a scam.

"Really?"

Shelly nodded. "Most tourists don't go off by themselves, even in the market. Like we are going to set upon them if they don't have strength in numbers?" She laughed, a pretty sound, like rain shivering down wind chimes. "Or they come in their big buses, and have tour guides they crowd after, men from the city who ride in on the bus, giving our history away as if it was their own." She shook her head and spat. "What do they know?"

"Nothing, I guess?"

"Worse than nothing. They know their version, their citified version of who and what this place is." She tugged Anita away from the market. "Like Santo Tomas. Come inside, experience it before we try to put words to it."

They walked up the stairs of the church, not an easy thing since people were burning some kind of piney incense on the steps, laying out marigolds, along with grain and fruits. The doors were open, and inside it was murky despite the many candles burning. Anita realized the murk was smoke. More incense. More flowers. From women working with altars on the open floor behind the few rows of pews and kneelers.

Shelly led her to the front, near the main altar, and they stood by the side wall. Anita was first taken by the smell and the smoke. She'd been in Catholic services where the censor went by, swinging the smoke of holy incense as the carrier walked. But this was different. More intense, more ... elemental.

"It is called copal, the incense they use."

Anita nodded. She recognized the marigolds, knew they used them in Mexico, too, for the Day of the Dead. The smell of them -- if there was one -- was lost in the fog of copal.

Anita nodded toward where an ancient woman held something squirming. "That's not a --"

It was -- or had been a chicken. Now it was dead, and the woman laid it on her makeshift altar, the blood soaking into the grain and marigolds in a bowl.

"What do you feel here?"

"I feel like this is something I don't understand. Like it is something ... other."

"Yes, it is exactly that." Shelly moved closer, talking low. "The guides, they will try to tell you this is some amalgam of Catholicism and the local Mayan culture. They will tell you that the church is benevolent, letting the pagan rites continue." She laughed low. "I will tell you they had no choice. They placed their church on top of a sacred site and the Goddess will out. What is hers remains hers, no matter who builds on top of it."

"The Goddess? Just one? I thought the Mayan pantheon was large."

"It is. But anyone who understands these things will tell you that gods and goddesses are but aspects of the great power. They make the universe easier to understand, by breaking it down into things humans can relate to."

"So you don't believe in them?"

Shelly smiled. "I didn't say that." She took a deep breath, as if she was breathing in the copal, the raw smoke that left Anita feeling a little light headed. "There was a priest here once, Father Ximenez. He understood the people. He understood this land." She took Anita's hand, led her back outside to stand at the top of the stairs. "Do you know what the Popul Vuh is?"

"I've heard of it." Which was only half true. She'd heard of a Popul Vuh Museum that was down the way from her hotel in Guatemala City.

"It is the book of our beginnings. The book of who we are. Father Ximenez translated it into Spanish, gave it to the world." She seemed very far away. "He was quite a man, the good father, to be trusted with such a task. A man who was not tied to absolutes." She fell silent, then laughed softly and shook her head. "He is a favorite of mine, historically speaking."

"I can see why."

Shelly studied her. "Why did you come here, Anita?"

"Why wouldn't I come here?"

"You are alone. This country, it has a reputation for being dangerous, no? So, you choose to come here?"

"I saw pictures. It felt ... it felt right." What it felt was far away from Jay. If it was dangerous, so much the better. Maybe she'd finally feel something again.

Shelly seemed to accept the safe answer. "Come, we will visit my favorite weaver." She led her down the stairs, past the hotel with its little splashing fountain that Anita could see through the open side of the courtyard. Macaws and other parrots flew around in the trees; flowers bloomed in a riotous explosion of color and tones. So many versions of pink, of red, of orange and gold.

"You like birds?" Shelly asked.

"I like animals."

"I, too, like animals." Shelly laughed and looked embarrassed for a moment. "I adore snakes. I know it is weird. And I have learned not to wear one on my arm when I approach those who seem like they might be open to the real tour of this town."

"Snakes are sort of ... ick."

Shelly's look turned stormy for a moment, then she took a deep breath. "If you knew them better, understood what they do, you'd know they are not ick, as you say."

"I'm sorry. I didn't mean to offend." Although she'd been being charitable with just ick: snakes gave her the willies.

As they walked away from the market, toward the trees that surrounded the town, a strange creaky cry sounded above them.

"The quetzal." Shelly stopped and scanned the trees, then pulled her in. "See, up there in the second highest branch of the third tree. A bird that puts macaws to shame."

And it did. Bright turquoise green and blue with a startling red chest, and long tail feathers that formed a train of sorts.

"Our money is named after it because the feathers of this bird used to adorn the cloaks of Mayan royalty and priests." Shelly's expression turned grim. "They are getting rarer, though, these birds. Man moves in, animals move out, until there is nowhere left for them to go." She nodded. "It has a prettier voice when it is not upset. But then, which of us does not?"

They walked on, and Anita started to get nervous. "How far is this weaver?" Every step took them farther from town, the market, and her driver. Anita suddenly had visions of waking up in a bathtub full of ice, minus a kidney.

"Not far." She glanced at Anita. "You don't trust me, do you?"

"I don't trust anyone right now." Why had she said that?

"Why not?"

"I guess I'm not a very trusting person." Which was a lie. She'd trusted Jay right up to the moment he walked out.

"Here we are." Shelly stopped at a small house. There was no door, just a blanket woven to look like a rainbow. Shelly pulled it back and indicated for Anita to go in.

Inside, the walls were covered with weavings, and huipiles were hung on a rolling bar, the simple shirts stark in their whiteness, the snowy fabric broken by the colored weaving that gave each one its own character. She pulled a shirt off the bar, saw that it was a rabbit chasing the moon, blood flowing down from where the rabbit's paws hit, flowing off the curve of the moon, too.

"Ummmm."

Shelly laughed. "It's not violent."

"Just like that poor chicken in the church didn't meet a violent end?" She could live her whole life without seeing another chicken's throat slit.

"This represents fertile womanhood. The blood is woman's blood." Shelly stroked the shirt. "You see how soft it is, how tight the weave?"

An old woman came in through the back door; she did not seem surprised to have visitors. Her eyes were glazed over with the milkiness of cataracts, but she moved around her room with no problem, setting up the back-strap loom easily. Then she waited, her fingers poised on the shuttle.

"What do you see?" Shelly moved closer to the old woman, touched her shoulder.

Anita thought it was a cruel question, given the state of the woman's eyes, but then the old woman looked up at her, and said something in what was probably Quiche.

"Isolation. Unhappiness. Pain." Shelly looked over at Anita. "I ask again. Why did you come to Guatemala?"

"To get away."

The old woman nodded and began to weave, leaning back and forth to adjust the tension on the loom, shooting the shuttle through the threads so quickly Anita almost could not keep track of it.

"Grandmother." A little girl ran in, calling out in Spanish, a large green snake wrapped around her arm.

"Look, I found one." She saw Shelly and held the snake up, earning oohs and ahs.

Anita backed away.

The girl smiled. "It won't hurt you. See." She held it up, the snake's forked tongue flicking in and out, the light from the open back door hitting its scales, finding blue and yellow in what had looked a flat green, making it seem like one of the old woman's weavings.

"It's okay." The girl reached out with her other hand, pulled Anita's hand toward her, then held the snake to her.

It slithered onto her arm. She expected slimy, but it was dry and cool, and as it wrapped itself around her arm, the sensation was almost soothing. She stared into its flat eyes, heard it hiss and thought she could hear a message in the sound, only she wasn't sure what it said.

The old woman said something in Quiche, and Shelly took the snake from Anita and gave it back to the little girl, then told Anita to come see the weaving. Startled, Anita looked over -- the old woman was done? How long had Anita been communing with the snake?

The old woman patted the ground next to her, and Anita knelt.

The weaving was a jumble of colors at the bottom, orange and green and blue, with red thrown in but not as much as came out later, at the top.

"Anger." Shelly knelt on the woman's other side and traced the red.

The little girl leaned against Anita's back, the snake hissing near her ear. It felt good, this closeness, the unfettered affection of a child.

Anita would have liked to have had a child. She'd thought she and Jay .... She'd thought a lot of things about her and Jay, none were going to come true.

The old woman talked in Quiche, hands following the threads that ran across the pattern. The traditional diamonds and crosses were missing; in their place was Anita's life.

A black patch marred the design. Anita reached out and touched it, and memories of Jay's leaving flooded her. He didn't love her anymore. He'd met someone new. He wished her well -- maybe they could still be friends?

More red flooded the weaving after that. More anger.

And then a change. A rainbow, rising out of the red. A snake, green like the little girl's, slithering up the rainbow and a rabbit waiting at the end of it, hugged by a woman sitting in the curve of the moon.

"I've seen this image," Anita said, rubbing her hand over the rabbit and the woman in the moon.

"Yes," Shelly said. "It's from the Dresden Codex. The goddess Ix Chel. Goddess of childbirth and motherhood, of the moon and the rainbow."

"A copy." She felt disappointment flood her. She'd thought the woman was making something just for her, had felt it speaking to her.

Or maybe she had just been desperate to believe that, to feel special?

"No. Chak Chel here has never seen the codex. What she makes is an original -- her original." Shelly smiled as if something was a joke.

"Don't be sad. This weaving is for you," the little girl said in Spanish, then took her snake and ran off.

"If it's for me, then what does it mean?" Anita was feeling angry again, felt the red inside her, like the crimson of the quetzal's chest, like the blood-red that covered her design -- if it was even hers.

"You know what it means," the old woman said in English, pulling the back-strap off and pushing herself to her feet with a surprising grace. "We each of us have pain. You must work through it. Find what you are meant to be and be that." The old woman pulled Anita to her, kissed her forehead and whispered, "Your life is up to you."

Then she walked out, leaving Shelly and Anita alone.

"Can I at least take this with --"

The loom was bare; no weaving on it, just the shuttle sitting between empty threads.

She backed away from it, bumped up against Shelly, who said, "You don't have to be exciting to be brave or interesting. But you can't live your life in your head all the time, either. Here, in my land, you have found the middle way, perhaps?"

Anita turned. "What have I done that's brave?"

"You rescued a parrot." Shelly smiled as if that were a great thing. "I'm very fond of those birds, so I thank you for taking care of it."

"How could you know that? Did my driver put you up to this?"

"Your driver knows of me, but he's never met me." Shelly turned her around, her arm around her shoulder like they were old friends as she steered her to the door. "Follow the path to town. If you see a green snake, don't touch it."

Anita frowned.

"You were holding a tree viper. They're venomous."

"What?" Anita had the urge to wipe down her arm.

"Brave. See?" She touched her cheek. "A little child made you brave. You will make a fine mother. And I know these things."

She backed into the house, the blanket slipping down to cover the entrance.

Anita pulled it aside, went back in. "Wait, I--"

The house was empty, no hangings on the wall, no rolling bar hung with huipiles for market. No loom. The back door hung half off the hinges. Light peeked in from chinks in the walls. She turned; the blanket on the front door hung in tatters, the colors of the rainbow faded.

No one had lived here for a very long time.

She heard the echo of a child's laughter, the hiss of a snake. She smelled copal again, filling the room even though there was nothing but the dust she'd kicked up.

Then the smell faded, it was calm and warm and quiet. She walked out, saw her driver coming up the path.

"Now you are exploring decrepit buildings?" he asked with a laugh. "Let me guess, there was a bird in need of rescuing?"

She laughed, too. "No."

"Come on, it is time to go. You found nothing in the market?"

"I'm not sure yet."

He gave her a look, seemed about to say something, then yanked her away from the edge of the path.

A green tree viper was slithering through the grass between two trees.

"I was playing with one of those."

"Crazy, crazy lady." He was laughing.

Crazy lady. No one had ever called her that. And she liked the way he said it. Not like something to be pitied, more like something to be admired.

"Thank you," she said. "Thank you very much."

Homecoming
Karla Linn Merrifield

She promised them she would return,
and did, a millennium later, in May.
She came home to red-faced cliffs,
to young green cornfields quilted
along meandering washes flowing
through tang of piñon, juniper, sage;
to flowers of yucca and prickly pear;
but mostly she came home to the Spire
of Spider Woman, towering beyond time
from valley floor to storm clouds.
She once sat there, listened, believed.
There the Woman taught her to weave,
not reeds into sturdy baskets,
not flax into colorful blankets,
but words into chants, prayers, songs
for her people, the long-ago ones,
whose songs are gone,
gone from *Tseyaa Kini*, gone from *Kinaazhooshi*.

But today she who is welcomed
by the old spirits with lightning, hail,
thunder, and rain; they are ever thankful
she remembers, is still the poet, Weaver-in-Words.

In this land, these Canyons de Chelly and del Muerto,
at *Tse Na-asshjee-ii*, in shadow of late spring evening,
shadow of ruins, shadow of echoes of the joyous lost,
she is again kneeling, praying, writing.

The Seasons March
Kit Koinis

They have so many things to say about death, most of them contradictory, and all of them confused. Perhaps it's because it's such a personal event that no one really can say what happens, but I certainly didn't expect it to come in the form it did for me. I've never been one to fear death, as someone who works so closely to nature as I do could never really fear such a natural transition, but it still came as a surprise.

It was an April morning when I first saw you, although I knew that you didn't reckon time the way I did and you would neither know nor care what month it was. You wouldn't pay any never mind to me, either, had we even been up face to face, but that was just fine with me. I knew that your kind was as joyously self-absorbed as any of my mesa friends, and you didn't mean anything by ignoring me, good neighbors as we all were.

I know it was April, because the first time we met, you were running off with a bolt of cloth – my best pillowcase, now that I think on it – just as fast as your little legs could carry you. I've often wondered if you'd taken off with my freshly washed laundry because you knew that I'd bear you and yours no ill-will. The way your kind always seem slightly huddled over with an insincere frown on your muzzles, you always did remind me of naughty children, caught in the middle of some prank.

At first, I thought you were a chupacabra sent by a spiteful bruja, come to make off with some of my chickens, but then, it was a rather bright green pillowcase, and I'd only spied you out of the corner of my eye. When I figured out just what it was that I was looking at, I laughed so hard, the flour from making sopapillas dusted all about me, temporarily causing a white-out in my own kitchen, thinking about how fanciful my first impression was. So it was that we began our relationship with laughter, a stolen pillowcase, and spring flowers scenting the desert air.

Your people have always been the night-loving kind, so I didn't worry that I didn't see you very often, and I didn't try to pry into your secrets, either. We were both content to let each other be, and for that, I think you made one of my better friends, unlike the roadrunners who would occasionally come over and spy on me with their little beady eyes, or the crickets who would keep me up nights with their constant music. Maybe that's why I was so surprised to see you, the next time.

I remember our second meeting quite clearly, maybe because the timing was so strange, or maybe it was simply a longer period of time. In either case, it was probably late July, because the penstemon and Devil's Claw were already out, seduced by the fiery heat of our brilliant summertime sun, dotting the fields with purple and yellow flowers and enticing the mariposas to come and play.

I was walking through such a field, visiting the hardworking plants on my spot of land, gathering the produce of their efforts, when I heard a strange yipping sort of noise. Knowing that my own dogs were lazing about in the cool barn, a smile flickered on my face, as I wondered if it was you. Following that sound, I walked real stealthy-like, hoping that my presence wouldn't scare you off, and, either it worked, or you just knew in your wise way that I meant you no harm, 'cause there you were, and with four little kits, too!

The talkative one who alerted me to your whereabouts had his brother's ear in his mouth, and it was all I could do to keep from laughing at the expressions on their faces. That's when your eyes met mine, and maybe it was the motherly spirit that we both possessed that allowed it, but it seemed as if we shared a secret smile between the two of us. You allowed me to watch your children stalk the fluttering insects that afternoon, a memory that's forever been burned into my heart. Watching them pretend that they were the fiercest of warriors as they attacked mariposa, each other, and my pants leg once, without the slightest sense of malice boys of my own race would have had, had they been playing these kinds of games, is a sight that I'll always be thankful for.

It could have been that the sweet tone of that early afternoon that made our third meeting so traumatic, but I think I would have been heart-sore from it in any case. It was late in our monsoon season, and the earth was squishy with rain it wasn't quite sure what to do with. Maybe it was the mud that slowed you down, or maybe it was simply that you, like me, were getting on in your years. In either case, the triumphant howls of my dogs alerted me that they had caught something, and I had best see which neighbor had run afoul of them.

I jogged as fast as my weary old bones would let me, and as I came upon my dogs, I saw that they had caught you, my friend. With frenetic energy, I shushed off the dogs, and gathered you in close, hoping that they hadn't harmed you too terribly. I pounded into my house, and quickly gathered the first aid kit that I kept on hand for events such as this, and did my best for you. Just as I finished suturing the long, angry gash in your side, the skies seemed to open up -- crying like a mother no longer able to keep her fears to herself. There were cracks of thunder that shook the house at times, and I knew that my garden's soil would be everywhere under the onslaught of the heavy rain, but never once did I leave your side that night. I think that that was the reason you pulled through.

I fed you on blue atole for a few weeks until one day you were simply gone. I wished you well, and I think my dogs learned their lesson, as they never did go after another of your people.

Our last meeting was for only a moment, but just like all of our meetings, it's been etched into my head and heart. It was last Christmas, and I had the taste of biscochitos and hot chocolate in my mouth, a reminder of the quiet repast I had just enjoyed. The snow was coming down in gentle little flakes, and I knew that I'd have icicles and a frozen walkway in the morning. The window above the sink was slightly steamed from the hot water where I was doing dishes -- the same window I had spotted you out of the first time, so many years before.

Looking back now, I'm not quite sure what drove me to look out the window -- maybe I just needed a change of scenery from the dirty dishes -- but I'm glad I did. You were walking down my path with a strapping young male who was obviously courting you, and the two of you looked such a picture, haloed in the light of my luminarias. I could only see you for a few moments, as I've said, but for those few moments, it seemed the world stood still, just as it's doing tonight.

I had been dozing by the fireplace tonight, when I heard a gentle scratching at my door. I sighed a little, and painfully stood, my muscles protesting in the cold. I made my way to the door, opened it, and there you were, looking as young and spry as the first time I saw you, making off with my green pillowcase. You came inside, for the second time in our friendship, and I knew just what you wanted. I bent down, my face to yours, and laid a bony hand upon your head, and for the second time, I felt your fur radiating warmth into me.

Like I said before, I've never feared death, but looking into your kind, all-knowing eyes tonight, I wonder now why I ever grieved about it.

Mt. Kailash

George H. Northrup

It is always cold here, cold and forbidding,
slippery snow and icy rock,
Himalayan air as dry and thin as death --
all part of the warning to be
as desperate for enlightenment
as a man with his hair on fire
is desperate for a pond in which to jump.
Otherwise, don't begin!
Here ponds are frozen, and the jump is astral.
Up and up from Lake Manasarovar,
climbing through exhaustion
on this seabed coral lifted to the sky,
Kailash wielding wisdom's hammer
far above my stubborn skull.

Here at the top of the world,
still and barren,
here at the top of the world's emptiness,
age-old truth is post-Newtonian:

nobody connected to nobody;
only the connection is real.

I would vanish *if not for these others*,
here in freezing nights, disoriented days --
Shakyamuni, trekmates, Sherpas,
even the Chinese border guards --
if not for these others
circling the sacred mountain
together.

Here physics reigns in radiance with metaphysics,
uniting cosmic and local.
Within these soaring, iridescent peaks
eons and ions empty into present fullness.

Say this without words, Kailash,
looming in pantomime.
Say it in stony silence
so everyone can hear.

Bargain with the Mountain King
Juli D. Revezzo

Frenie wiped the sweat from her brow as she scanned the Arizona airport. People glided through on their way home, or to business meetings, and she searched the commons for some sign of familiarity. Uncle Morris' assistant Alan promised to meet her but she didn't see his brainy, scrawny figure anywhere. She retrieved her bags from the carousel and sought out her cell phone.

"Alan Lessings," he answered, his smooth tenor voice a little shaky.

"I'm here, Alan," she said. "Where are you?"

They met five minutes later by the Starbucks. Alan took her bags from her and led her to his car as he explained. "Last saw him Tuesday night. Everything seemed normal, but by morning, I found his room empty."

Frenie scoffed. "There's no secret in that story," she said. "Did you check with the newest, prettiest research assistant?"

Alan glanced at her out of the corner of his eye. "Come now, your uncle's the perfect gentleman."

She snorted. "Depends on your definition of the word gentleman, doesn't it?" He had a knack for drinking the wrong things, chasing after the wrong women, and angering the wrong boyfriends. *Gentleman* was the last thing anyone called him. Even his students used his honorary title lightly.

Alan didn't agree or disagree. He set her bags in his trunk and she settled into the passenger seat. He reported their last night while he drove through town. Nothing out of the ordinary. A few femur bones turned up in their dig -- they were well on their way to confirming the tribe they'd found was Celtic, just as some of the locals claimed. Alan spent that night typing up their notes and in the morning, found Uncle Morris gone. Frenie snorted. "Maybe he intended to fly home and cut you out of the scoop."

"Whatever he meant to do," Alan said, "he didn't make it."

Frenie shook her head. "You know, the news had some crazy story this morning about a headhunting cult out here."

"Well, the Celts did do such things."

She snorted again. "According to some fifteenth-hand accounts. Don't tell me you think a headhunter got him."

He shrugged. "Who knows? Maybe fairies spirited him away."

She tapped her nail against the window, watching the city fly by outside. "Maybe they made him their king."

Alan remained silent, and she looked over at him. His dark eyes narrowed at the street outside.

"What's wrong?" Frenie asked.

"Headhunting cults." Alan snorted. "I'm afraid that, at least, isn't too far from the truth."

Surprise punched her in the chest. "What do you mean?"

Alan turned off the road and they rumbled down an unpaved path. A tall structure of dark stone rose ahead. Three legs supporting a slab of smooth granite. He parked before the formation, and slid out of the driver's seat.

"Nice place," Frenie said as she surveyed the site. "This is where you work?"

Alan nodded, then shook his head, as if not sure how to answer. Frenie narrowed her eyes at him. "What's wrong?"

Alan pointed to the structure's opening. "Look."

She approached the structure, gazing up as the monstrosity rose over her head, higher and higher as she neared. She wondered how many local tribes had once used this as a place of worship, or a burial marker. Excitement made her want to step inside, and she quickened her pace.

Yellow police tape shone sharply, like a bright scarf caught across the entrance. A bright *Keep Out!* sign she didn't need to see to heed. The mere aura of the structure made her shiver. Beneath the police tape, a round white rock.

No. As she came closer, she saw it for what it was. A head. Strips of flesh scoured off it, the skull showed white beneath pink streaks of blood and sinew. Shaking, she ducked under the police line. And then she paused, gasping as she recognized what was left of the face: a curve of cheek, and a thin beard shaved to a point, like Uncle Morris used to wear his.

***

Night brought the strangest dreams. A man sat on the tip end of the desert dolmen. Green robes flowed around his feet as he gazed down at her. Feathers and some strange script decorated the neck and sleeves of his coat. Were these the robes of a local native priest? Or the gown of an escapee from the local insane asylum? Frenie wasn't sure. He wiggled his finger at her, beckoning her to come sit beside him. Why? The man was a total stranger, just as this landscape was foreign to her. Dry, dusty Arizona had nothing on the heated wilds of Bermuda she so loved. The dream scared her awake. Why did he beckon her? What did he want? Who was he?

The morning sun rose and at 6:30AM, she snatched up her cell phone and called Alan. "Get your gear together. I want to see the site again."

He argued and cajoled, but Frenie would hear none of it. She had to find out more, must understand how Morris had gotten here. And why she got the feeling she knew everything about the stranger in her dreams, despite the fact that she'd never seen him before.

The site shone in the morning glow, the sun's angle highlighting different features in the rocks than she'd noticed the night before. The hues more brilliant, the purple shadows deeper, the golden and russet soil and rock brighter -- and she didn't wonder why they'd named this place the Painted Desert.

The dolmen stood out like a smudge of black eyeliner under Mother Nature's eye. She approached it, eyeing the police tape and the blanket now covering the spot where the severed head had rested. She glanced over her shoulder to see if anyone official watched and when she was satisfied no one was looking, she crept closer to the dolmen. She kicked up dust as she scuffed her boot across the ground. The police tape wafted in the breeze. She sniffled, fighting back a sneeze, and leaned into the dolmen's entrance.

She sighed in thanks for the shade and peered into the darkness.

"What the hell was he doing in here?" She ran her fingers over the rough rock. "At night, what could he see to study?"

Who'd been waiting for him to perpetrate such a heinous crime? What Alan had said about headhunters crept back into her mind.

Frenie shivered and turned her attention to the incisions in the rock face. "Is this writing? It's not Spanish."

"Nope," Alan said from behind her. "Not German or French either."

"Then what?"

"Damned if I know," Alan said.

Frenie pursed her lips and continued her visual sweep, spying nothing out of the ordinary. Just sheer, old, cold rock.

"Not used to anything like this in the Triangle, doctor?" Alan asked.

"Not usually," she said. She knelt and crawled inside. The entryway proved a tight fit. She couldn't straighten her arm when she reached overhead. How had Morris' head ended up here?

A light flashed inside, small, indistinct, then gone. The light flashed again. This time, it glowed from beneath her. She wiggled into the shaft a little further. "You've got a lightning bug trapped up in here." She crawled a bit further, feeling the path slope gently downward. The light shone again, always out of reach, though.

A warm breeze wafted over her. "*Shew!* That's some lightning bug. Never knew they gave off heat."

But not enough light to properly illuminate the darkness. She reached into the pocket of her vest and pulled out her flashlight. The walls around her glowed golden in the beam, and in its light she spied spirals. "They incised this thing on both sides," she said. "Did you know about this, Alan?"

No answer came. She reached up and ran her fingers along the spiral. The stone crumbled beneath her touch. The roof caved in. Frenie crossed her arms over her head and shouted for Alan.

***

When Frenie opened her eyes, she found herself in a brightly lit cavern. Torches burned in braziers along the walls. Bison skulls hung along the walls; puma skins covered the floor. No approaching sound came from above. She could no longer hear Alan's voice. Had the police pushed him back? Were they trying to get help for her?

She gazed at the bison heads again, taking in their once-impressive horns, and cursed her luck. She was hot, and now tired. And her butt hurt, and here she was in some underground ritual nightmare. She pushed to her feet and walked to the far side of the room, scanning the walls, seeking the entrance through which she'd fallen. Large, heavy boulders sat immovable in its place. She cursed to herself. How had this happened? She swung her gaze around the room and spotted a second passage. She jogged to it, rubbing her pained backside. Spirals and three-armed triskeles decorated the stone's perimeter, but the passage itself stood dark and foreboding and though she leaned as far as she could inside and shouted, she received no answer but her own echo. If the passage led anywhere, she couldn't see its end. Would it be prudent, or stupid to climb inside?

Given her previous experience, she wasn't so sure, just as she doubted where she was.

"Alan!" she shouted up the passage.

Nothing. Frenie spun on her heel, leaned heavily against the wall, and fished in her pocket for her cell phone. She flipped the top open.

The glowing display screen read: *No service.*

She scoffed as she slapped the top shut. "Hell." *All right, Frenie, think.* She wasn't a rock climber and she wasn't claustrophobic, but she hesitated to try climbing back into the passage. What if she wedged herself in? What if she died in there?

She reached for the canteen she'd clipped to her belt that morning, only to find it'd had somehow disappeared.

Jesus! Now she wasn't only to die of stupidity, but thirst as well.

Somewhere in the distance, soft chimes clanged. Frenie spun and leaned into the passageway. There, a light glowed. That blasted lightning bug again?

"Hello?" Frenie shouted. "I'm down here, whoever you are!"

Again, her call went unheeded.

What are you afraid of, ghosts? She wiggled into the shaft. She'd been working in the wilds of Bermuda for years now. She'd trekked through the Serengeti in her youth, and got lost in the Scottish moors once when she was seventeen. *You can do this.* She shimmied up the shaft a little further. *You never once lost your wit. Why should this be any different?*

"Because it's tight and enclosed isn't anything to worry about."

Bison heads and old religious carvings meant nothing. Whoever had abandoned the place had left long,

long ago. There was no one here to worry about. Getting stuck here, on the other hand ….

She clenched her teeth and wiggled up a little further. "Just because the cops found Morris' head outside, why should that bother you?"

"Does it? How oddly you people take invitations these days."

On hearing the deep voice, Frenie gasped and went still.

"In my day, such offerings were charms to bring in the good."

Frenie spun in the shaft to find a man smiling at her from the entrance. A dark beard covered his thin jaw. Eyes swathed in darkness watched her intently.

He reached out a long-fingered hand to her; a dark sleeve falling forward couldn't hide the glint of silver at his wrist. "They helped to keep the odd ill omen away, too. Men have forgotten how to use them. Sad, isn't it? What are you looking for in there, Miss?"

"Who -- " Frenie's voice shook as she tried to speak. "Where did you come from?"

"I might ask you the same thing," the man said.

The man smiled and offered his hand. Frenie slid forward until she sat at the edge of the tunnel. "There now," the man said. "Isn't that better? Come. We're about to begin."

Over his shoulder, she saw the once empty room was now elegantly decorated. Tapestries covered the walls, chairs carved in intricate spiraling designs stood here and there around the room; a vast array of candles flooded the cavern with light. A table filled the room, almost from end to end. Its shining cherrywood surface bent under the weight of the succulent dishes waiting there. The sweet scents of yeasty bread and honey and sugared treats mingled with the tangy scent of the roasts lining each. A hint of rosemary and other herbs lay under the aroma somewhere, too, she thought. Frenie's mouth watered and hunger made her agreeable. The stranger laid a steadying hand on her arm as she slipped out of the shaft.

Music filled the room.

Frenie's feet hit the floor. The surface gave in as if she'd landed on thick, soft grass. A gasp of surprise escaped her lips.

People milled around the cavern; some carried platters, depositing them on the already heavily-laden table. Others lit more candles. Some of the women sprinkled rose petals around the perimeter of the room. They wore diaphanous gowns of soft flower petals; the men wore vests woven of the finest wool, and slim pants tucked into finely tooled leather boots. But of the musicians, as yet, Frenie saw no sign.

"Come," the man's voice drew her attention back. "We don't lay this feast just for ourselves. It's for you as well, our guest of honor."

The urge to call out to Alan gripped her. She rubbed her eyes. This must be a dream.

But no, when she opened her eyes, the scene remained. The enticing scents, the music, the princely, handsome man, studying her; all beckoned her. Could she turn back? Should she?

Frenie looked from the man's hand, to his handsome smile, and taking his hand, she slid out of the tunnel.

The crowd cheered. Frenie laughed. The music swelled. One of the women clapped her hands. The workers set their tasks aside save for one who carried a goblet to her. As Frenie took the goblet, something tickled the back of her mind. A warning, maybe -- or a dream. She shrugged off the feeling and sipped the cold, sweet liquid. A veil shimmered between she and her escort. He seemed at once more familiar, and kingly. She offered the cup to him, fighting off a cough. "What's the celebration for?" she asked.

"In the new tongue, some of your people refer to it as Litha."

"Pretty name," Frenie said. "Early summer, yes?" She felt a blush climb up her cheeks. "European festivals aren't my forte. You'll have to speak to my uncle, Morris, if you're interested."

He held her gaze and for a moment. She wanted nothing more than to stay here, and in his arms, forever. Why had she come, again?

He set the cup aside and whirled her into the flow of the dance. "I'm more interested in you, Frenie," he said.

"Who are you?" she asked.

He shushed her, and whirled her around once more. She hummed the tune, at once sure she knew it like she knew her favorite song and perplexed at where the tune might go next.

"I'd like to know," she insisted. "And, where am I, comes to mind."

"Some call me king, some call this home." He kissed her hand. "I care more about your opinion of the second than the first."

As he whirled her around and around the circle, she couldn't get a grasp on the structure. Was there a table there, a door? Did curtains hang to the window sides, letting in the moonlight, or the sunlight? Did she see the Arizona skyline, the rainbow-bright hues of the desert, or the blue of Bermuda's gulf waters? Or the green hills of England? Or the deep dark, browns of an Irish bog? The dance made her head too dizzy to process it all at once.

"I think it's lovely," she managed to say.

Another man took her hand and spun her away from her escort. Only a few beats passed before her escort stepped in between them, and pulled her back into his arms. The dance kept her rapt as well as it kept her confused.

"Tell us a story, lass!" someone shouted.

"Yes, a story of your lands!" said another.

Which lands? she wondered.

"Tell us of your island," said a third.

She took a deep breath and met her partner's eyes. "If I'm going to tell stories, I need to bow out of the dance, sir."

She stepped away but her escort pulled her back. His eyes glittered with mischief. "Who says? Let's try something else: Tell me your story and I'll decide if it's fit for my guests."

What story would satisfy them, she wondered. "Well," she said, "there's a naval dockyard there that Benedict Arnold's son built."

"The traitor's son did something for them?" someone said. "Trying to pay off a Debt, undoubtedly, sir!"

Frenie shrugged. "Who knows what his true motive was."

"Tell me something else about it," her host requested.

"It gets fairly warm there in the summer, in the mid 90s," she rattled off statistics. "Then there's the hurricanes, so I'm lucky if I get any time to work in the summer. I only flew out because Alan called me."

"Out here, you mean?"

She nodded. "Well, with Morris' death -- "

"And who's he?" someone shouted. "Ah, she's got a lover, sir!"

"No!" she protested.

"He's your family. And family keep their promises, don't they?" The king whirled her in another spiral and as she faced him again, he stopped her, both hands on her shoulders. "I ask again: What -- "

She couldn't make out what he said next, his words garbled in the flood of sensations. "What did you say?" she asked. "What's the question?"

"Tell me why your uncle resisted my request."

What did he ask Uncle Morris? Why would her uncle forbid him anything?

For a moment, her giddiness fled, and fear tightened her chest.

"What did you come here for?" the king asked. "I realize, it might not be as pretty as your island but -- " He leaned closer, close enough to kiss her. "If you could, would you live here?" he said. "Could you be queen here?"

She shook her head. "Forgive me, but unlike other little girls, I never dreamt of being a queen."

The room dissolved away and she found herself standing on the peak of a purple crag. The red desert floor spread out before her several stories down. The wind whipped at a red shawl draped now over her shoulders, entangling it with her skirt.

"This was your dream." She found the king stood beside her now, wrapped in a white mantle trimmed with fur as crimson as her shawl. The reverse of what she might expect to see Santa Claus wearing.

Below them, she could see the barrow's entrance, and poor Uncle Morris' head.

"That," she said waving a finger to the gruesome scene, "was never part of my dream."

"But it was part of the breaking of the bargain."

Frenie clenched her shawl in rigid, cold fingers, glaring at the king. "What bargain?"

For all that he hadn't moved an inch he seemed to loom over her, his fingers entangled in her hair and stroking her cheek. "You know the bargain of which I speak. My realm is in need of a queen, Frenie. Do you not now know why you've come? Truly? Do you not remember?"

His smile lit up eyes as golden brown as a field of wheat. A hint of infernal red flickered in their depths. The feeling of a hand reaching through her chest and squeezing her heart gripped her. She didn't know whether to move closer, to accept him, or jump -- and where would that leave her if not in a similar state as her uncle?

She shrank away from him. "Dear gods!"

He laughed. "There aren't many gods here, not ones who would look kindly on the breaking of our bargain."

"I don't care for their kindness!" She shook her head. Was that really true? And was it something she should say here? In this holy place?

What did it mean if this wasn't a place she deemed holy?

Jump, her mind said. Run away. What if she died here, on this unhallowed ground? What would her family do? Would Alan be able to understand what had happened here? Was he down below, waiting? Would they ever find her? Would they find her like they'd found Uncle Morris?

She glanced again over the edge of the rock. Damn, but it looked like a long way down. She could barely make out the skull. Several figures milled around the base of the dolmen, ants to her eyes. How far up did the dolmen extend? She could've sworn it wasn't so high before. She gasped and stepped back as some inner primal instinct kept her feet firmly planted on the outcropping.

She took a deep breath and turned back to the king. "Give me the terms of the bargain. Let me see if I can't match them."

A smile curled the edge of his lush lips. "You know them, Frenie. We laid them out together, many years ago."

"We did?" She blinked, her mouth agape. Speechless, she took in his brown eyes, the contours of his cheeks, the elegant curve of his wrist where he fisted his hand against his hip. Waiting. The mass of red hair billowing out behind him on the evening breeze. The glowing nimbus surrounding him had nothing to do with the setting sun, nor the glow of celebration torches.

Her world shifted again and she tumbled down the dolmen entrance, or felt as such, falling head over heels. She landed feet first, and stumbling, slapped a hand against the warm stone of the garden wall.

"Careful, lass."

He was there, too. He caught her arm and studied her face, his not so different than in the Painted Desert. Only it rose above her from a different angle. Frenie snatched her hand out of his and bit her lip. "I'm such a klutz," she said. She paused, wondering at the sound of her own voice. It hadn't been so high in years -- decades.

She straightened and took in the scene: she puttered in a small garden. Her bearings righted slowly, the circle around her narrowing, taking on the outlines of her familiar world. She chuckled to herself. What an odd dream! She took a deep breath: earth and rose.

The petals, soft under her fingers, rustled in the morning breeze. She sighed, stepped back and picked up her tiny watering can. Frenie remembered this. Spring break, 1991. Ten years old at last, and this was her first flower garden, a pot or two only set to the side of Mother's kitchen garden, but they were hers. A geranium here, a daisy there. Easily sown, easily cared for.

As her watering can's little pink spout poured its glistening nourishment on the beloved flowers, she saw a black, baby grasshopper creep up the stalk. It settled happily at the crux of leaf and stalk and began to munch.

Anger and annoyance took her and she bent and flicked a finger at the pest. The grasshopper flew through the air, undoubtedly startled at this disturbance to its lunchtime plans. It soon landed, shook itself, and eyed grass shoots nearby with a hungry gaze.

Frenie frowned down at it. "Of all the -- " She kicked at the bug. "Get out of my garden!"

The grasshopper hopped once and back towards her flower. She raised her foot and stomped down on the pest. "I warned you." She jogged to her home's back wall and flicked on the water faucet. "I did warn you, after all."

"I suppose you did."

She turned to see a boy sitting at the edge of Mother's garden. He wore green shorts much cleaner than most boys wore on days like this. His shirt sparkled with some special fabric she was sure his mother mostly kept for special occasions -- like Easter Sunday.

"Hello," she said. What was he doing here? She couldn't remember having met him before. "You're new in the neighborhood, aren't you?" He must be.

"You'd say so, wouldn't you?" His amber-eyed gaze scanned the garden. "But you'd be wrong."

Frenie snorted. "I've lived here all my life and never met you."

"There are few who take note of me. Apparently, you have a gift."

She set her watering can down and crossed her arms. "You talk funny." He spoke like no one she'd ever met before, despite some of the Hispanic children in her class. His accent was much different, rolling, musical. "I'd remember if we met before."

"Would you, now?" He swung his feet. "You met my family, yet you don't remember that."

Frenie bit her lip. "Is your mother Isabel?" She waved a hand to the south. "Two doors down, maybe?"

He shook his head again. "Nope."

She knelt and dragged a finger over the face of the garden gnome at her feet. "You're Jan's cousin." She nodded west. "She said she had family in France."

"Wrong again," he said. "Third guess, then no more."

"I don't remember saying we were playing three guesses."

"It's fun this way."

Might be, she thought, if he wasn't intent on annoying her. She shook her head and standing, took up her watering can again. "I don't wanna play. I'm busy. We can play tomorrow." He was cute, after all. She might not mind seeing him again. "What school do you go to?"

"Don't go to school. Not like yours."

The preparatory school, then. So, what was he doing here?

"Frenie!" her mother called. "Are you done yet?"

She peered toward the kitchen window. "Almost!"

"Do you need anything?" Mama asked.

"No. Just getting rid of a pest."

The boy scoffed.

"What?" Frenie asked.

"Which pest?" he said. "Me?"

"Yes. Shoo!" She waved a hand at him. "I gotta do my chores. Come back tomorrow."

"Things to do, people to kill," he said.

She whipped around to stare at him, puzzled. "Kill? I don't kill people. I'd never kill anyone. You get in trouble for it, bad trouble."

"Eventually." He leaned over to one of mother's roses, and held a hand out to a leaf. When he sat back he held up his hand, showing off a small, yellow-striped black grasshopper.

Another pest? Frenie sighed. She'd never succeed in caring for this garden. She stepped forward.

Seriousness overtook him and the smile faded. "Eventually, you do. How many of them have you killed now, little girl?"

Frenie stopped in her tracks as if struck by a tiny arrow. "What?"

He raised his hand as if offering the insect. "These. They're my kin, you know."

She rolled her eyes to heaven. Oh, he was not so much all there. "Right. If you say so." She turned to the next geranium pot.

And found the boy standing before her. She couldn't remember seeing him move from Mother's garden.

"You didn't answer my question," he said. "How many have you killed?"

"I don't know what you're talking about."

The boy reached out a hand, wrapping it around hers. The cricket leaped onto her wrist. "You do. How many?" he snarled. "How will you pay for it?"

The world spun. Frenie dropped to her knees. Something settled heavy inside her chest. She could barely breathe. Sparks lit at the edges of her vision. She watched the tiny creature leap unto her flowers and begin nibbling the soft petals. Then another, and another. She rubbed her eyes. The grasshoppers changed into a small woman in a black dress, and a man in a tuxedo.

The heat, that's it. The heat was getting to her. She reached out for her water bottle. Where had she left it?

"What did you say?" The boy leaned closer to her, shaking the water bottle mockingly. "Did you give me a guess?"

He shook the bottle. And the little people danced around the flowers. The world shifted around her. "I don't know," Frenie said, bewildered.

"How many, lass?" His eyes, she saw, were the color of dried grass. He narrowed them and opened his empty hands. "Ten? A hundred?"

Her breath came in short pants. "Maybe," she gasped. She stumbled as she rose. Tried again, dusting her hands in success when she got her footing. "So what? They're only bugs."

"Only bugs." He cupped his hands around his mouth. "Oh, Mrs. Mayfield!" he called.

Mother appeared on the threshold. "Yes, dear?" She paused a moment and looked from Frenie to the strange boy, and turned back to Frenie as if she hadn't seen the boy. "Do you need more water, sweetie?"

Frenie winced as the boy nudged her. "Watch this." He closed one eye and pinched his fingers together, moving his hand back and forth. It seemed to Frenie as if he sighted a dartboard. One more flick of the wrist and he opened his fingers.

Mom gasped and raised her hand to her forehead. She stumbled and rested against the doorjamb, sliding down to sit on the stepping stones, heedless of the dirt and water droplets staining her jeans.

"Mom?" Frenie forgot her companion and rushed to her mother's side.

Mom closed her eyes, sighed and opened them again. The boy giggled as if this was the funniest thing he ever saw. Frenie clenched her fists and glared at him. "Don't just stand there, do something!"

"Why?" he said. "You didn't, did you? When they pleaded, did you help?"

"What do you mean?"

He paced along the beam of pine surrounding Mom's garden. "You take mine, I take yours. That's the way it goes."

"Then I'll give you something in return!" Frenie cried.

The boy paused in his walk. The corner of his mouth curled in a strange smile. "You?" he said.

She blinked. "What about me?"

"You take my kin, I take you." He shrugged. "Or your mother. Either one. Doesn't matter. You'll both suit for my kingdom. You will come, and you will be welcome."

***

The music whooshed loud in Frenie's ears, pushing the past back where it belonged. The room swam into focus, though the light was much dimmer than the sun had been a moment ago. She blinked at her partner. "You!" she said. "It was you all along." That was why she studied archeology, why she dug in the dirt for already dead things. The thought of bringing some living thing harm haunted her dreams from that day forward. Even now she did what she could to avoid harming any insect, a worm, or any other being. She couldn't risk it. She couldn't risk another faerie, or god, or whatever he was, coming to accuse her of murder.

She pushed him away. "Enough of this. I've got to go."

"Are you sure?" he said.

"Yes." As she examined him, she could see features of that little boy in his face. If this was not her nuisance visitor, they must be related.

"Then he was right. You would not keep the bargain." He shook his head. "Frenie, I thought you'd tired of this now. Shall we go see your mother?"

Her eyes grew wide, then narrowed. "No." What did he offer on that long ago day? His kingdom? What did it mean? She crossed her fingers and took a breath.

No. He'd know if she lied. Somehow, she knew that.

She uncrossed her fingers. "I'll do it. I'll do as you ask."

"You'll -- " He didn't fill in the blank.

She gulped. "I'll be your queen."

A cheer rose up, the people resumed playing their music. Their spinning dance went wild around her.

"So be it," the king said. "The bargain's fulfilled."

He kissed her forehead, and the room spun.

Frenie found herself skidding along the passage. She stumbled, rolled, and came to rest at the entrance of the cave. Alan stood over her, staring down at something. She sighed with relief. Her journey ended where it had started. Was there nothing in the cavern after all? She refrained from looking back. She pushed herself to her feet and dusted her jeans. "Alan?"

He didn't hear her. He quietly knelt down beside something. A gust of breeze blew across her face. Why did he loom so far above her? Why did she stare at his knee? "Alan, what happened?"

"Damn it, Frenie," he said. "I didn't bring you out here for this to happen."

"What happened?"

"What the hell am I going to tell her family?"

"Don't know, sir," said another voice; a man she didn't know. He stepped forward and she got a good look at his shiny black shoes. "The whole family has bad luck," he said.

Alan scoffed. "That won't help, officer. She'll want more explanation."

The officer shrugged. "We'll figure it out."

Figure what out? Frenie wondered.

"Yeah," Alan said. "Meanwhile, how do I tell her mother we found Frenie dead, here?" A groove in the dolmen glowed blue near his feet, a spiral, rolling and rolling along, eon after eon. She didn't know whether he saw it, even though Alan cursed under his breath. "It's my fault she's here. I never should've called her."

The words rang in her ear. "*Deaddeaddeaddead.*"

Had Morris too found his way into this courtyard of gods? Had her journey across the gulf, across the US, been real? Had her trip underground happened? Or was it all a dying dream?

"*Deaddeaddeaddead.*"

The spiral glowed brighter. She could hear a faint, soft whisper. Even that died away. Then she felt a hand on hers. The darkness receded. The cavern lit up again with joyous laughter. She stood before the congregated people, each one glowing with light she couldn't explain. The king stepped in front of her, a circlet of twisted gold and green in his hands. He raised it high, and lowered it gently to rest on her head.

"The queen's journey is ended," he said. "The bargain's fulfilled."

Frenie ran a hand along the tips of the crown, feeling thorn, metal, and crystal graze her skin. She brought her hand before her eyes to see crimson blood and ash staining her fingertips. The wound knitted itself together instantly and she stared at her skin, blinking, barely able to speak. "… I suppose so."

The king kissed her hand, and winked a mischievous wink. "As I promised it would be. Welcome home."

Some Kind of Orpheus
Valentina Cano

Leaving you behind

has become the only option.

And no option at all.

I've dug into the underworld itself

for the key that would spring

that lock of memory open,

but it's lost,

drowned metal in that long,

black river

you've ripped open between us.

Into the Light: Safe Haven, 1944

Ruth Sabath Rosenthal

> "And you that shall cross from shore to shore ... are more
> to me and more in my meditations, than you might suppose."
>
> Walt Whitman, "Crossing Brooklyn Ferry"

Thank God for you, *Henry Gibbins*,
ship of dreams laden with bedraggled brethren
dark and fair, tall and short, all frail-boned and gaunt,
each and every one a survivor
reborn in the wake of conscience.
Blessed, their leader, Ruth Gruber; praised,
her leader, Franklin D. Roosevelt;
and you, Captain Korn
-- commanding officer extraordinaire --
your kind face and outstretched arms,
the ship's crew -- their smiling faces, helpful hands;
the stalwart bulk and hallowed halls,
sky-crowned decks surrounded by sea-speckled rail
-- far cry from barbed wire.

A joy, the glistening white toilets, toilet tissue;

divine, clean fresh air that fills sunken chests, lungs

ashen from the fires of Auschwitz-Birkenau, Bergen-

Belsen, Buchenwald, Dachau, Treblinka ...

And you, buoyant sea, revered for strong currents,

changing tides, gulls that glide the breeze

and assuage wounded spirit;

and you, huge dining hall bejeweled with vegetables,

cornucopia of meats, kaleidoscope of sweets that swell

shrunken bellies, smooth withered souls.

"Are you America?"

Soft pillows and ample blankets nestled in tier after tier

of bunks, the nightmares you help smother,

sweet dreams you set in motion;

the talent shows, chess tournaments, movies, musicales.

"Are you America?"

Oh, most wondrous throng -- my ancestry --

it is *you* who are America, *my* America!

Space Journey

Kristen Camitta Zimet

"We have been sending the wrong people into outer space.
We need to send a woman poet."
— Marianne Moore

Earth is dropped from us like a husk,
and we her naked seed, cast out
in the infertile night, move on,
making love to a sky we have never known.

The Archetypes are gone -- the sea, the rose,
the talismans we carried under wraps.
We have lost language, that tense necklace
strung between familiar stones.
We can touch neither end of any metaphor.

Earth is the man beside me, nothing more.
And you beside me, are you still a man
whose feet hug no world? Once we were defined
by what contained us, flowed to us,
what we flowed out to greet --

Earth's air, ancient with exhalation,

her answering pressure upward on the feet.

But here we meet not even the small,

carefully disposed litter of our days.

Here the deaf engine sobs in our ears.

Your voice (so little it takes)

shakes my invisible bones.

Time sloughs off like segments of the ship.

Time fails slow like oxygen consumed in a sleeper's tank.

Time is the frequency of speech with you,

the pulse of your unsteady glances toward me.

Turn! You are my single season and my mirror.

I am made in your image.

Now as we fall together toward the moon,

I am the moon:

the side of me turned toward you shines.

Read a bright desolation there --

a moon's cry down through sundered centuries.

Fall toward me now, my Adam, in this night;

meet me at last on heaven's empty knees.

[Originally published in *Frontier: Custom and Archetype* (Pig Iron Press, 1996).]

Myself to Myself

Scathe meic Beorh

A mist that reminded Hilda of clouds lay close to the grassy earth where she walked. She moved with slowness, unsure of her steps, for she did not recognize the land. "I feel good, though," she said to herself, trying to build her confidence. "I feel as if I have slept well, and am ready for the day." It was then that she saw him, sitting at the riverside on an outsized stone. His legs were crossed, both feet tucked beneath him. His face was covered by a hood of a cloth not dyed, but she could see part of his long black beard. His hands, draped about his knees, looked strong; weathered. A bowl of salted fish and bread sat next to him. Hilda trusted any man who sat with such confidence.

"Sir?" she said as she stopped, placed her feet together, and folded her hands in front of her. "I am looking for my mother …. Do you know the *hlæf-dige*[1] called Alvi Stormursjávarsíða? I am her daughter, Hilda. My father is the *hlafweard*[2] called Blad Starkbeväpnar. Do you know him?"

The stranger turned his face to Hilda and smiled. She took in a quick breath of surprise, for she had never seen such eyes -- eyes like swirling woad pools -- nor such peace upon any countenance.

"I am pleased to meet you, Hilda Bladsdóttir. I am the *hlafweard* Frälsare Gudson."

"Do ... do you know my fólk, Hlafweard Frälsare? And, will you tell me where this place might be? I have somehow gotten lost. I have awoken only a few moments ago, you see, and, while I slept, someone has moved me to a place I do not know."

"Are you normally picked up and moved while you sleep, Hilda?"

"When I was little, yes, but not now. I'm too old to carry around. I have already begun my ... my womanhood. *Oh!* I'm ... I'm sorry ...." Hilda's hasty words made her blush and turn her head away.

Frälsare said nothing, only held out his hand for the girl to come sit next to him on the stone. She inched forward. "Come," said the warrior. "I see something in the river that may tell us where are your fólk."

"You are a seer, Frälsare?"

"Some have called me a seer, yes. Come. *Sit*. I will give a young woman room enough of her own." The lord slid to the edge of the stone, providing Hilda with ample space to feel comfortable to sit with him. She did so, and found that she held no fear of him whatever. His body did not threaten hers. She felt only tranquility with him.

"You are so calm, good sir."

"Some say that as well."

"How can a warrior such as yourself be one of such calm? My father is good to his family, but he is a violent man in his love for us and for our people. My mother, same as that. No one crosses our threshold with fire in his eyes and maintains that fire."

"Strong fólk, Hilda, sounds to me. But many nightmares."

"Sir?"

"Look into the waters as they run by. Close your eyes and tell me what you see."

Hilda shut her eyes, but was taken aback by what she saw so that she opened them again in quickness and grabbed the arm of Frälsare to steady herself lest she fall from the rock.

"What did you see there, my lady?"

Hilda has never been called 'lady' before. She felt cared for by this strange warrior Frälsare. "I … I saw six warriors coming across the river, carrying two people whose … whose throats were cut. Blood poured forth as if their deaths were new."

"A party of armed men numbering less than seven are thieves."

"I know those words. That is a saying of my father."

"An old saying indeed. Who were the dead you saw?"

"I do not know. I could not see their faces."

"Will you look again? Be not afraid, Hilda. I am here. Keep hold of my arm, if you wish."

Hilda closed her eyes. Being of tough stock, she kept them closed as she wept and said what she saw. "The six warriors, two of them shield-bearing women ... come toward us as if walking over the waters -- a magic feat I have never heard of before. Across the shoulders of the strongest two men are thrown ... are thrown ... a man and a woman. I still cannot see their faces."

"Enough, sweet girl. Open your eyes. You have seen enough."

Hilda coughed. Blood filled her mouth and spewed over the front of her white over-dress. "Something ... wrong ...," she said as she fell into the arms of her new friend.

***

"*Vakna*, Hilda. *Awaken.*"

Hilda opened her eyes. She felt hungry. Frälsare gave her salted fish and bread. She ate with hardiness. She stood. Her legs were strong. "Did I sleep?"

"You slept, but now you are awake. There is a pool of water just there. No breeze blows. Go and see yourself in it."

Hilda went to the pool. She dropped to her knees. Her fingers savored the coolness of the long grasses where she knelt. She looked into the pool at her reflection. She cried out at what she saw, and recoiled. She fell backward. She scrambled across the ground like a wounded animal.

"What do you see?"

"My ... my throat! It has been cut!"

"Yes. Last night. As you slept in the house of your fólk."

"But … the six warriors I saw on the river?"

"*A party of armed men numbering less than seven are thieves.*"

"We … I … do you mean … that I and my fólk were … slain by thieves? As we slept? Slain by the six warriors I saw … *oh!* Was it my mother and father they carried? Where are they now? Where are my fólk? Was it my mother and father who lay dead on their shoulders?"

"Come with me, Hilda. You have much to see."

"Where are we? This place is not my home! *I want to go home!*"

"Does this place not look like your home? Do you not recognize that yew tree just there? What about the riverside here? Does it not seem a little familiar to you? And those hills just there. Have you not climbed them many times?"

"Maybe. But … I have never heard of you, Frälsare. Who are your people? And … why do you dress as you do? You do not attire yourself like the men of my land. I also see now that you are not armed! You do not even carry a spear! I see not even a belt knife with you. Yet … your hands … they are weathered as they should be, yet soft like those of a woodworker. Do you work with wood?"

"I did, as a trade, before I began my true work."

"What do you mean? What is a *true* work? Is not work what a man or woman does in life?"

"Have you heard this poem, Hilda?"

"Which? Say it."

"I know that I hanged,
on a wind-rocked tree,
nine whole nights,
with a spear wounded,
and to Odin offered,
myself to myself;
on that tree,
of which no one knows
from what root it springs."

"Yes. That is the word of All-Father Odin. We were being hurt by the witch called Heidi. She wished to destroy mankind. Odin saw no other way for us to be saved than to sacrifice himself on the majestic yew tree called *Yggdrasil*. He pierced his own heart with his own spear. Then, when he came back to life, he had with him a runic *godspell* that saved us all."

"That is a beautiful story, Hilda."

"It is a true story. It really happened."

"I should know," said Frälsare as he pulled his shirt from his belt and showed Hilda the wound in his side.

"My ... my g-god Odin?"

"If that is what you wish to call me, yes. *I am*. The Beginning and the End. No one comes to the All-Father except through me."

"Then ... who are you?"

"To Odin offered,
myself to myself;
on that tree…"

[1] 'loaf-kneader' or bread-maker; origin of 'lady' (Old English)

[2] 'loaf-ward' or loaf-keeper; origin of 'lord' (OE)

[Previously published in *Eternal Haunted Summer*, Summer 2013]

I shall set free my hair and wear a fawn skin

Rebecca Lynn Scott

This is the dead time, the mad time, the empty time, the parched time. The time when my own mind turns against me, and all I want is a deep dark cave with a trickle from one of the great rivers at the back of it, or the sweet release of shedding everything of the daily world to run wild in the night.

In Greece, the dead time, the time when nothing grows and Persephone reigns beside her husband in Erebos, is the summer. Grain is planted when the autumn rains begin, and harvested in the spring when the rising heat turns the barley heads to gold. The idea of her time in the Underworld being winter didn't come about until people in more northerly climes began telling the story, because of course for them, winter *was* the dead time.

I grew up in Florida, where summers were either hot and very dry, with wildfires and smoke and the parching sun; or hot and wet, with mosquitoes, sometimes disease-bearing, breeding in the stinking standing water, and hurricanes. As a child, of course, either sort of summer just meant not going to school and splashing under the sprinkler, in somebody's pool, or in the ocean. The only difference was how much sunscreen versus how much bug repellent, how much smoke versus how much wind.

But as I got older, summers got worse and worse.

I have bipolar disorder. High school was when it started getting serious, although I wouldn't be diagnosed until college. And that's when summers started to get bad. I spent as much time as possible hiding from the sun, staying in the air conditioning, swimming only at night. And year by year, it got worse, until I spent five or six months a year desperately depressed, feeling stretched thin and dried out. (In Florida, summer runs May through October.)

Somewhere in there, as I became more deeply involved in the worship of Hekate, I discovered that summer was the time when nothing grew in Greece … and suddenly, things made much more sense to me. I had never put it together before, that summers were so bad, that the heat and the light were doing this to me, that this happened every year. August was always the worst, when it got so bad that everything had an unreal, dream-like quality, a play watched in a cloudy mirror, everything at two removes and out of reach.

As I came to terms with my bipolar, I also began to worship Dionysos as god of divine madness. It helped me come to terms with it, not only that it would always be a part of my life, but that I needed to treat it. Divine madness, I came to learn, must be sacred in the most etymologically literal sense: it must be set aside, it must be something taken out of the daily world, like the space within a Circle. I could not live there all the time, and I could not let it rule my life, not if I had ways to control it.

I moved away from Florida, to Seattle, where summer retreated to less time and less heat, and I could set aside the madness more cleanly. There's more light, and my sleep cycle flips around almost completely, and for days on end I curl up in my light-blocked, air-conditioned bedroom, leaving it only when I must. But those days are fewer, and the span in which they happen is narrower.

In the dog days of summer comes Hekate's time, and then sometimes I spend days in a light trance, where everything has more meaning, and every choice leaves ripples. I walk her white roads under the sun, and her silver roads under the moon, and her secret roads when the moon shines not at all, and while all of that is often true in my service to her, August is when I am most aware of it, that I am hers.

But Dionysos remains, and as I study him more, I understand better his connection to Persephone and the seasonal cycle, and I make ritual sense of my disorder. And the journey he sets me on, that he invites me to join him on, is very different.

Dionysos has always been connected to Persephone, although today, as most people reduce the myths and the old stories to those found in Hamilton and Bulfinch, we have lost much of that connection. It's still there, though, if you go back to original sources.

Once, there were two Dionysoi, and the elder was called Zagreus or Euboleos.

Conceived when Zeus, in the form of a mighty serpent, visited Persephone before her marriage, Zagreus was set upon Zeus' high throne with thunderbolts for playthings and weapons. The Titans (urged on by Hera in her jealousy) stole in upon him and dismembered him with knives, though he fought valiantly. Athene carried his heart to Zeus, who made from it a liqueur and gave it to Semele, princess of Thebes, who became pregnant with the next incarnation of Dionysos, and was inspired by Hera to beg a boon of Zeus, and that boon was to see him in his true form and glory. She died of it, and Zeus rescued the demi-divine fetus of Dionysos and sewed it into his own thigh, to give birth to him yet a third time, now fully a god.

Or else the Dionysoi were called Dimetor, of two mothers, and their births were separate and unrelated, and Zagreus, the elder, still died, and his deeds were attributed to the younger, and they were worshipped as one.

Or perhaps there was only one Dionysos, born of Zeus and Semele, raised by the nymphs on Mount Nysa or Euboia or Naxos or Sparta, and he was Persephone's brother, and retrieved Semele from Persephone's underworld. He made Semele immortal, and named her Thyone, and set her amongst the stars, from which she came down to join him in his revels, a goddess of madness and joy. Or perhaps it was his wife Ariadne whom he rescued. Or both.

Or maybe Zagreus who became Dionysos was a chthonic god, and was the son of Hades and Persephone, and his rites and gifts came to mortals from under the earth, where Persephone was called the Mother of the Vine.

But always, always, Dionysos, elder or younger or only, is the son or the brother of Persephone, and always he visits her. Because madness, even divine madness, without transformation, is a trap, and journey with no ending, only endless whirling to the beat of drum and flute. But with Persephone's transformation and rebirth, the madness becomes a journey.

The journey through madness, which shucks off the burdens of everyday life and frees us (for Dionysos is called Eleuthereus, the Liberator) is a journey of dark as well as of light, and we may walk through Tartarus as easily as Elysium. While we journey, led by Dionysos Agyieus, Dionysos of the Ways, the path leads down as well as up, and we walk in the keeping of Persephone Chthonia, who knows the fear we feel when we begin to venture from daylight's paths, for that fear is a fear of oneself. If you do not know yourself when you drink the wind and pound the drum, you will come to know yourself as you travel down, and Persephone has sympathy with that. Through Persephone comes all transformation and all rebirth, as Dionysos himself was reborn, and so through the transformation of madness and the rebirth of recovery, she touches us and holds us.

Sacred madness can take us beyond trance and ritual into a place where meaning ends, and there is only being, only doing. Freed from the chains of the rational, we revel, unafraid of ourselves. We dance in the wilderness, where there are no roads, making our own roads where none can follow without madness.

To descend into madness without Dionysos of the Mysteries, madness that is not sacred, is to be lost, to be trapped on an annular path that never reaches Persephone, to be held back from the transformation and rebirth that she brings. That is the madness that comes from my body and my brain: a cage and a chain, not freedom. It is not set aside from my life, but infects it, as mold infects grapes, spoiling them for the pressing, so that I can take no joy from my life. The madness of my body becomes something to be endured and waited out, a stopping, not a journey, and from that place I call out to Dionysos for aid and release, to Persephone for transformation, to Hekate to light my way when I can see no road out. It is a slow heedless meandering off the paths of the known, away from what is loved, without noticing the growing errancy until it is too late, and I am lost, with no notion of where I am and no map to get home. If I am lucky, I can still hear the voices of my loved ones calling me home, of my gods telling me the way, and if I listen to them and trust them, and do as they say, I may yet come safely back. Or I may wander in the unrelieved and meaningless fog indefinitely, stagnating in my own mires, for years on end. I have gotten better at listening, better at noticing when my footsteps wander unintended. And sometimes, just sometimes, I can choose to dance in that place of concealing mists and brackish waters, and by doing so forge paths that bring me back closer to myself.

The sacred madness is a journey I take of my own will, down into the depths and up onto the heights. This madness is one that is chosen, a dance I must mean to begin, a deliberate step off the constrained paths of the familiar and the mundane I must take in order to travel the ways that do not exist until I have danced them. Through wine and song and dance I travel, moving through the madness as it moves through me, allowing it to change me, to rebirth me in a way that brings me back to my life fresh and renewed, able to take up my burdens again, remembering how to be free of the fear of myself. Every step, every note, every beat, every sip changes me a little more, becomes a drop in the rising tide of transformation, until it becomes a vast wave in which I do not drown, but on which I am lifted and by which I am purified. Through Persephone the Transformer I am reborn, and through Dionysos Soterios, the Savior who brings us recovery, I am returned to myself, my journey complete.

Returning to myself, I find that I am washed clean of the anxieties and fears that plagued me. They'll muddy me up again, soon enough. This journey was not to change them, but to change me. Being clean and free of them for this small time, I can choose how and when to pick them up again, how to arrange them in the pack on my back so they balance better and chafe less, as this journey ends and I return to my mundane journey, much refreshed. And so the cycle begins again, mundane world, madness and transformation and rebirth and return (a journey even the god has made), and then back the the mundane. But every one of those small cycles moves me further along the journey of finding balance with my bipolar disorder, making peace with it, as I must do again and again, as it, too, shifts and changes and transforms.

Passing Through the Portal
Elizabeth Bodien

You have led me to this strange, desolate place
-- windswept impasse between towering rocky cliffs.
You let me bring what I thought I needed --
my burdens drag behind me in red, swirling dust.

Legions await your command across distant plains
and on violet seas beneath these dizzying heights.
The air is full of signs, a mantle of your presence.
As for me, I have come as summoned.

Now you ask me to leave my burdens at my feet,
to ignore this baggage of my years --
grey regrets, jagged sorrows, prismatic joys,
even my seeing, my hearing.

You ask me to give up everything,
to carry nothing, to empty myself
like a bowl. I am trembling.
Nameless, how would I know myself?

Red dust eddies in the whirlwind.

This sky spins colors I have never seen.

I'm no longer sure what is me, what is not.

Words disappear and then …

Walking the Labyrinth

Kristin Camitta Zimet

It sounded quirky and highbrow for my staid little town. The purple flier announced an Autumn Labyrinth Walk. People would be welcome to walk a replica of the pattern that is inscribed on the floor of Chartres Cathedral. For four thousand years, the flier said, labyrinths have aided meditation. My Sunday afternoon was booked, but I would spare this oddity a few minutes.

Outside the church gymnasium, I took off my shoes, amused that they had set the Labyrinth indoors, in so secular a space. But inside were altars to the four directions -- tables with cloths and candles -- and in the center, a huge expanse of white canvas painted with purple lines. A woman glided to my side, to gentle my way in. It was good that she did, because I balked.

Labyrinths loomed in my memory. There were the schoolgirl mazes we labored to draw, our smudgy paper full of snarls, pitfalls and dead ends. There was the funhouse maze made of glass and mirrors at the amusement park, where I stumbled about bashing my head, as my family laughed. The maze in my childhood mythology book, where the beast laired in the middle ate prisoners. The hiking trails that did not fit my map, so that I limped back into the same intersections as night closed on the forest. The wooden pens at the high school lab where my brother ran rats, then locked them back up. Mazes to constrain, delude, deny passage. Mazes to addle the wit and quell the spirit. Mazes to taunt, *get out if you can*.

But my guide was promising this one was fail-proof. "The way out is the way in," she said; every point on this labyrinth lay on the true path, the only path, between the exit and the center. Besides, there were no barriers to sight; I could just walk across and off. She would watch me the whole time. Indeed, if I liked, she would walk with me. All she asked me to do was open myself to the experience. I stepped into the Labyrinth.

The going was tiresome. The loops around me gave rise to hateful images, a butcher shop hung with sausages, intestines fallen from a wounded belly. I concentrated on putting one foot in front of the other. When would I get to the center? My will pushed to the center: to master it, to arrive. It was, I recognized, the way I charged into all experience. I went headstrong to achievement -- at work, at love, even at pleasure. I gave myself migraines. I tied myself in knots, mazes of anxiety. But wasn't that also my finest gift? I could hurl myself straight, with all I had, at what I wanted; I could knock down what stood between me and my heart's desire.

Now I moved more slowly, testing the ground. When the path I was on ran straight, I said, how hungry I am to get somewhere; when it doubled back on itself, I said, how hard it is for me to yield a little ground. I felt my eyes running ahead to discover whether, in moving aside to allow others to pass, I had failed to return to the right place on the track, in which case I could be trapped after all. Maybe I was circling. I did not trust the pattern -- and there I began to cry. I had never in my life trusted the pattern.

Suppose I did trust: suppose it was enough to set one foot before the other as the way opened: suppose nothing else had ever been required of me. It would be restful; I longed to try. But I hung back. I would champion my own style. I asked, with my whole self, *should I not run to what I seek, like a lover to the beloved*? Answer came back, not in my ear but direct to my middle. I heard, *not that seeking which mars the finding.*

And then I did yield, content to follow the pattern. A moment later, lifting my head, I was dumbfounded to see that I had arrived at the Center.

* * *

I spent a long time at the Center, suffused in warmth, surety, power that required me to run nowhere and do nothing. But I began to grieve that I would have to go, to begin the long retracing to the outside. Grieving began to spoil being there. I saw that anticipation of loss had slowed my way inward, too, had always pushed me back. Like desperation, it had marred the finding. I took hold of the grief, hugged myself tight, and walked out of the Center.

People had been passing me, heading both ways on the one path. I had felt the passings as awkward kinks in my pattern. Now I began to feel the people themselves, moving at various points I had traversed, like fingers plucking notes across a harp. There was in fact a harp playing, which I had been tuning out. The harpist was repeating a Scottish folk song, the one about Bonny Prince Charlie sailing into exile from his kingdom. So was I. I saw that many of the others were crying, for their own reasons.

For the first time I stopped focusing on my own progress and position. I looked at all the walkers. Together we formed an atom, each of us curving around one center at our needful speed and distance, our energies humming. We might be one body, made of world on world of atoms on interlocking courses. Or a universe, the same design on a wider canvas.

One grey-haired woman was moving lightly, almost skipping. I had laid so heavy a significance on each footfall. I tried her way, and the doublings back were much easier, like a hawk wheeling on the wind, around an unseen center. I sent unspoken thanks across the design. I looked out across the pattern for my guide, to thank her too. I would ask for her later, when I got out.

But I was already out. I felt the same shock of surprise as I had on reaching the Center. The way back had been so short. It struck me: the way in was the way out. If it was so short a trip from Center to edge, then the blessed Center must be very close, accessible all the time.

At once I wanted to go back, to test this out. I would try trust again. But I teemed with doubts. Did needing a second time prove my distrust? Would repetition be "seeking which mars the finding"? I might go back to find the power less. Joy might have an extinction curve. I had always doubted love, figuring I would wear out my welcome.

* * *

I did walk into the Labyrinth again. This time the music floated me. I saw that the design took me at once very close to the heart of the Labyrinth. Indeed, it was made so that I walked closest to the Center at the very start and farthest out just before arrival. I stopped thinking about distance; I enjoyed feeling that however the path turned me, I echoed the curve of the Center itself. The folds lay embracing the Center, like a robe lapped around someone's feet. They spread like concentric ripples outward from it. Delight sped me. I found I was in the Center, and the power and peace were as before.

I would not sully this moment with loss. I asked, with all my being, a question which I could not have framed before: *may I take this with me*? And felt at once the answer: *behold, I have enlarged you.*

For the second time I began to walk the Labyrinth outward. I went drawing the joy behind me along the path, like a golden train, like a wedding gown. As I walked the Center itself grew larger. The way out was the way in. I saw small curves facing outward all along the outermost line of purple paint, Centers everywhere at the supposed edge. There was no point that was not Center.

At the so-called exit I turned, opening my arms to embrace the Labyrinth and my sense of wholeness. There was no pang when I went to retrieve my shoes, and faint surprise when I saw I had been there three hours.

At the door my guide met me with open arms. I hugged her, and words proved unneeded. She exclaimed, "Oh, you are changed!"

[Originally published by *The Labyrinth Society* in 2004.]

She Who Holds the Reins
Brenda Kyria Skotas

The journey begins with a choice.

In a way, it is the choice itself that initiates and proves the change to come. For none who choose to take up the sacred roads can find the end unchanged.

One who walks such roads is Hera.

Though she is Queen, immortal and all powerful, she is known for setting foot to earth and walking where the mortal kind live and fall. She is responsible for the quests of many. Her name is on their lips as they journey, whispered numbly, in madness or in pain; and it is her madness still that greets them at the journey's end.

Hera is a goddess of trial, though the motives behind the ordeals are often unclear, and frequently derided. These trials, be they great or small, are the most sacred of journeys. From the labors of Herakles, to the emancipation of a beaten wife, they may begin with a prayer or a single word, but always they begin with a choice.

Somewhere there sits a woman, eager for change, for a chance, for the power and courage to be something more than what she has been. To be something other than the role she has been forced to walk. She whispers into the darkened sky, eyes fastened to a streak of stars, and she speaks the name of the Queen of Heaven. The syllables are hesitant, but as they are shaped between her lips she feels the cold cloud of the goddess settle around her, a single shiver in an otherwise warm night. She may not even realize as the eye of Hera finds her. Her heart is stirred, and in her mind she sees the road ahead. She knows what it is that must be done if she wishes to find her way out. Perhaps she doubts or hesitates ... maybe her heart shudders in fear ... but the path is made clear, and it is in her hands to choose her fate.

That second offers her a choice, whether to take up the road and the challenge of the Queen to find her way along the journey, or to remain and forget her aspirations. This is the moment where all potential hangs. Here in this choice, with the far-seeing eyes of Hera upon her, a journey is already begun.

Hera's names are many, and her hands have touched every soul. In two aspects we find Hera as the guide, she who reveals the path ahead, where journeys may be found or finished:

She is known as Hera Prodroma, and her feet race over the earth. By this title she is one who walks ahead, the one who guides and scouts the paths to come, that she may direct the best suited roads.

She is known also as Hera Heniokhe, and it is she who holds the reins. By her fist she guides both chariot and steed, and she breaks the lines opposing forward march.

It is important to realize that these aspects are not filled with tenderness. She will show you the way, but she will not help you to walk it. It is a very particular journey that Hera is guide to. These are journeys reliant on the self, the most sacred journey of the soul, be they spiritual or mundane in detail. You may always choose to accept or decline the challenge set before you, but if you accept the journey to be upheld, it is up to you to see it through, to failure or triumph, neither end greater than the other.

I have found that with Hera, the journey itself is often where the lesson lies. She will set before you a path to walk and the goal is often seen in reflection sometime after the fact, even when you've stumbled and necessity has sent you back from whence you came.

She is not the guide who is the gentle mother, but she who watches all from on high.

It is she who is Queen, who chooses to set foot to the earth and to learn the roads and names of mortal kind.

Her ways are not always clear to us, for her vision is wide. She will not give you the answers to your struggles, but she will reveal the paths by which they can be found.

Persephone

Valentina Cano

One look in his eyes and the flowers
she'd pressed to her hair crumbled to ash.
The black ink of his pupils
widening at her face,
pale,
a moon in the day time,
he fell back a step.
Then two.
Opening a channel between them,
slicing a vein across the floor.
She shuddered like a tree in winter,
all her hopes plunging to the floor
like dead leaves.

Walking Two Worlds
Larisa Hunter

I wake in the cold, dark soil and question how this began. I never thought my life would take this turn. How could I? I began so simply. I walked into Heathenry through a complex series of paths. When I began, the idea of wandering here, into the underworld, was not something I intended. I began my journey in the land of Frigga, a cabin surrounded by lakes, with thick fog floating in reed-filled marshes. There by her spinning wheel, I sat content with my life. Carding wool, sipping tea, I was safe. It was warm, embracing and glorious. For over three years I listened to her. She would tell me about her children, the worlds of the Gods, and speak to me in ways that only a mother would. Her kindness, her love, surrounded me, enveloped me and made me whole. This was my upper life. It was the world of the Gods merged into my daily life and it was magical and blissful and wonderful.

When I became pregnant she was the one who shielded me, comforted me, and held me through nine months of waiting. I saw her there in my labour pains, smiling, encouraging, and singing. She made me believe I could do this, and gave me every ounce of strength. It was the best time in my life. Motherhood is a precious gift. With my babe in my arms, I would dream often of what she would grow into and how lucky she is to be surrounded by the gods of my faith. Blissfully, I slept, with few worries, and it was glorious.

Then the weather began to shift. Without much warning, I started experiencing abdominal pain. Being the woman that I am, I ignored it. I went about my life, as if doing so would numb the pain. If I just kept going, kept walking, kept sleeping, Frigga would carry me through. Around my daughter's third birthday, my journey began to change. As snow falling on the green lush grass, the world shifted. I began my sleep the same as every night, but this night would be far different. This night, I found myself not in the comfort of Frigga. A dark cloud seemed to surround my sleep. This night, there would be no tea, no comfort, no laughing. This night would be something completely unexpected.

As if out of a nightmare, I felt a hand on me -- on second thought, not a hand, but a bone ... raw and pointed, skeletal without skin, it hovered on my stomach and in one movement it dragged its fingers across me, etching a six pointed Hagalaz on my stomach. I woke to check my stomach, but there was nothing there. Just me, the room, and my sleeping husband, all normal.

But things were shifting within me. I felt compelled to get checked out. Something was wrong, I knew it, I felt it, it was clear. No more fooling yourself, no more denial -- there must be a reason for the pain. A trip to the doctor led to a trip to the hospital for an ultrasound. The wait for an answer was agonizing, as my mind was filled with doubt, while life dragged along with little thought for my worries. After a few weeks I got a call: "You might have cervical cancer." Two months later I found out that I had endometriosis. Endometriosis was less frightening than cancer, because it was not life-threatening, but it was painful and debilitating. It became almost impossible to live with the pain. After the diagnosis, talk turned more and more to a surgical solution: removing my womb. Thus began my descent.

The idea of removing my womb was a devastating blow, and I resisted. I wanted to keep it. I had always hoped to become a mother again, hoped for a chance to have another child … but it was not to be. I felt like I would be losing myself, like I would be losing a vital part of me and my power. In my vision, I stood on the edge of my glorious fertile fields and peered into the depths below. I found myself wondering what this would mean to me. Would I lose all of myself? Would I still be me?

This is when the ground began to tremble under me. The world of Hel began to creep ever closer to my green marsh. One day, I entered Frigga's cabin to find Her there, Hel Herself. The Queen of the underworld sitting with a cup of tea, one skeletal eye open … staring. She offered me a chair, which I took. A staff was put on the table. But this was no ordinary staff: it was made out of bone, and not just any bone, but human bone. They both just stared at me.

At this time, the mood of my dreams began to change. I would wake in the underworld, scared and shaking. Surrounded by snow I would wander for hours, lost, alone, and weeping. Hel would talk to me, scold me, and encourage me. The time spent there changed me. I began to see the underworld differently. It grew less scary, less imposing, and I began to think that there was a reason for my being there. In my waking moments, thoughts of what was taken consumed me, and I found it hard to be happy, despite the lack of pain. But something within me was transforming. Every night, I would go into the underworld and I gradually began to make sense of things.

I researched the role of women in Nordic societies, as well as the role of a particular type of woman called a völva. The more I read, the more I wondered whether I was meant to take on this role. Was it my destiny to be initiated like this? I was not certain I wanted this, and found myself at odds with my faith and my Gods. Heathenry does not allow you to deviate much, and it certainly does not deal well with 'prophetic' visions. But, here I was, already a GodsWoman, an author and more, but not really ready to become something else.

My dreams turned almost nightmarish. I woke in Hel in flames, flesh being purged from my body, falling onto the ground, weeping in fear, and yet out of the ashes I rose. This was merely the beginning. The following trip, I found myself embraced by Odin and stabbed through the heart, left for dead, confused and disoriented, calling for help, but none came. There was no understanding, no reason … just pain, death, and rebirth. Then, as if I could bear no more, I woke in a frozen field, beside a grave, beaten, bleeding, surrounded by gods, and left to die. These were only the beginning of my body being pushed to the edge of death, beyond it, through it, and somehow surviving it. My living world became one of exhaustion. I prayed for release, prayed for help … yet there alone in the darkness … there was only silence.

These experiences were quite frightening, but there was something to these journeys beyond the fear. The transformations were like being washed clean, becoming something new, changed, repaired and reborn. The underworld kept calling. Hel would just sit there for hours … staring at me … peering into my soul. The road became easier, and my dark, dank underworld became more like a home. The nightmares became more like coveted lessons, and I drank the cup of Hel for several months.

I sought an explanation in my research, and there, as if waiting for me, calling me, offering me the answer, I found the myth of Gullveig:

> She remembers the first war in the world
> When Gold-Brew was hoist on the spears
> And in the High One´s hall they burned her
> Three times they burned the three times born
> Often, not seldom, but she still lives!
> She was called Bright One when she came to the
> > settlements
> The greatly talented Carrier of the Wand

> She performed magic, ecstatically she performed it
> She knew how to cast spells
> She was always loved by wicked women.
>
> -- *Voluspá*, st. 21-22
>
> ("The Vision of the Witch")
>
> in the *Poetic Edda* (Kvilhaug)

It struck me that I was not alone. I was being transformed. Into what, I still had no idea. I doubted the push to this life of a völva, even if it was persistently calling me. The more I searched, the more I found which called me forward. "Here" they called, and led me to first this book and then the next, opening my eyes to a world in which I found myself at home. I saw myself in these dreams carrying a staff, like the women before me. I was changed, transformed and born ... not only a woman, a mother, a wife, but a staff-carrying woman, a völva. I had survived my trials.

With Hel by my side, I had found myself a friend, a companion, an equal. She who dragged her icy fingers onto my belly, who had borne me pain, became like a sister, a true friend trusted and loved beyond anything I could imagine. The darkness of her world became my womb, and there I grew, became strong, eager to take up whatever request she whispered. Once again, my journeys resumed a measure of comfort, and once again I found myself free of pain, of longing, and of solitude.

Spring arrived, and there I was again at the house of Frigga. I ran to her, hugged her close, and shared my tales of terror. I recall her sweet hands about me, holding me as a mother holds an injured child. I was home. As I stepped into her house, the room again familiar, I turned to see that staff, that staff of bone, again sitting there … but this time … it had a strand of white thread, and a rune of Frigga upon it … and there again the face of Hel greeted me, but this time there was no fear, no desire to run. This time I sat with her and Frigga, reached out my hand and took up the staff. I had accepted the new life that I would live.

Now my feet walk two worlds. I am of the green, the mother, the wife, the confident author and GodsWoman, but also of the dark, the mystic, the spiritual seeker. No longer mistress to one goddess, but to two. I was no longer defined by my physical parts, but had become something else. My dreams now return to the happiness with which they began, as I wander the nine worlds with the wisdom and grace imparted to me. It was them, those fine ladies, who taught me that *you are you, and always have been. You did not lose yourself, but gained us. The pain, the torment, the loss, all of it was felt by us, just as it was by you. In those moments, alone and bleeding, we were there, we saw you, we believed in you, and you survived.*

It was that one word -- survived -- that struck me to my core. I knew that from this moment on I could and would survive just about anything … my death gave me life. I searched for a way to say thank you, to give Hel and Frigga both my 'womb'. I knew I had to say goodbye to the life of fertile mother, and knew that this gift was theirs; they earned it.

I symbolically took an egg out and said in the most confident words I could:

I give this egg to Hel, as a symbol of my womb.

Hella,

You take much,

But reward greatly,

I know not what path you wish me to walk,

But I am listening.

Frigga you asked me to take up a staff,

Hel you gave me one of bone.

I therefore, before my kindred, take both.

To walk where Hel takes me,

To listen to Frigga who calls me.

I take this distaff and thread,

And declare myself theirs.

In this act, I finally committed to this road with the greatest of humility, prepared to do my best. My journey was not one that was desired or wanted but it changed me. It made me realize that my fear of what lay in the underworld was unwarranted, that embracing death and being one with these periods of initiation served to make me into something stronger. I stand here now, a year after my surgery, and think of all I have been through, suffered through, and triumphed over, and do believe that I can get through anything! Becoming one with that warrior self means being a woman who can traverse multiple roles just as I walk multiple worlds.

Baptism in Four Reflections
Craig W. Steele

1. Submersion

Unspoken fears have risen to plague all my endeavors;
corruption breathes within me, consumes my very soul.
When hungry ghosts come calling, I hear accusing echoes
reflecting darker egos, beyond my mind's control.
My heart is sore and feeble, entangled with depression;
I need to understand *Me* to banish hungry ghosts.
I slip beneath cool waters, descend beyond safe limits,
enraptured by the struggle to exorcise the host.
I contemplate salvation and journey where I must go,
discover what I must find, reviving dying hope.
Suspended 'tween two worlds now, surrendering my lifeline,
I'm floating like an island, deserted, yet alive.

2. Emergence

Upon the face of waters, winds pirouette in circles,
uplifting waves at random, creating art with heart.
Just underneath the surface, new power springs unleashed as

a waterspout shoots skyward in living, drenching rain.

Soon all across Creation, from deep within the darkness,

there swells a mighty music from faces in the deep.

A spirit wind is surging above the face of darkness,

and stirring all around me the bones beneath the bones.

I travel in my mind's eye, awakening my heart's light,

to find the *Am* that *I* am and cross the narrow place.

Enriched by dawning mind light, escaping my enigma,

I'm free now, out of darkness, to journey in my life.

3. Immersion*

All hungry ghosts fall quiet, for long, but not forever,

but now when they grow hungry, I feed them just enough.

I have reclaimed my life force and nothing circumvents me;

I am the *Am* that *I* am; I travel freedom's Way.

I know the Name of all things, remembering things forgotten,

and taking joy in living as Name and Being join.

Unbounded light flows through me, like rainbows in a sunbeam

without a destination; the Journey is my Life.

And when I think I'm through it, then something new arises --

there's chaos on horizons that I cannot foresee.

Enlightenment grows stronger, embellishing the brightness
reflecting vague half-shadows from gold baptismal founts.

4. Resurgence

My senses flow with focus, fly thoughtlessly with lightness,
and understand the silent, sweet language of a stone.
I cross the line unbroken, returning to the One Source,
and journey on across the Horizon of Rebirth.
I travel through the tunnel, both mortal and immortal,
towards a shining beacon embracing *All That Is*.
Time flows in rivers round me, like waters in a whirlpool,
no ending or beginning, as *Always* ever *Is*.
Awaiting my own judgment, at peace in my at-onement;
becoming as I once was and as *I* always *Am*.
Redemption, resurrection, revival of my Oneself,
no longer *being* me now because I have *become*.

*Poet's Note: Immersion is the state of consciousness where a person's awareness of physical self is diminished or lost by being surrounded in an engrossing total environment.

Nine Lives - A Feline Cosmogony
Literata Hurley

The parents of the first litter were the Queen and the Old Tom. They loved each other, and out of that love came life. Their four kittens were the first among the powers, and they came together to make the world. Then the Queen and the Old Tom took form within that world as the lights that alternated watching over it by day and by night, him blazing with light and warmth, and her waxing and waning like the eye of a great cat that winks at existence.

Each of the four embodied the spirit of a season and throughout the course of the year they took their turns bringing their particular gifts to bear. First came Miu, the maiden of the spring, with the gentle purr that coaxes the seeds into sending forth shoots. She gave way to Mrowr, the lady of summer's warmth, who was as red as a flame with bright golden eyes. Third came Kiri, as blue-grey as the rain and fog of Autumn, who lulled the world into quiet again.

Now last of the four came the Young Tom, the spirit of Winter, who was pure white with one blue eye and one green eye. As he looked at the world, he thought that the gifts he brought were least important of all. He looked at the love between the Old Tom and the Queen, and between his sisters, and he felt least-loved. In time he grew to hate the love between the Old Tom and the Queen, and he turned his eyes, his mismatched eyes, away from that love, and closed his heart to it.

In looking for something other than love, he found hate; in looking away from Life, he found Death that comes out of balance. He invented something new, and brought it into the worlds: he brought Death that comes out of balance, untimely, or because of hate, and he brought hate, the negation of love and life that desires destruction of another.

He brought these new things to the worlds, and wrought much grief and destruction through them. He made the darkness and the night times of fear, times of doubt, and he made the winter a time when it seemed that the whole world was wrapped in death. His sisters mourned and wept over the results, and they rose up and raged against the Young Tom and his creations.

They fought with him, and they sought to inflict his own inventions upon him: they hated him and sought to kill him. They threw him down, and he rose up; they threw him down again and again, and he rose up every time. His ears grew scarred and ragged, and yet he would not die a final death. They defeated him seven times, and their rage grew until they called on the Old Tom for his assistance. Neither they nor the Old Tom would ask the Queen to raise her paw against her own kit, but the Old Tom fought.

Mrowr, the spirit of Summer, joined with the Old Tom to warm the world, to drive back the cold and the darkness and the Young Tom who was at their heart. They succeeded in killing him again, but they could not remove his touch and his creations from the world. They could not warm the world too much, for the sake of the life that was on it, and they could not eliminate the Young Tom forever, and they knew that he would rise again.

Then the Young Tom thought that he would attack the Queen. He rose up and went to the Queen, and he declared his intent to her, to attack her, and to destroy the love that he felt had ignored him. She did not shy from him. Then he was curious, because she did not turn from him, and she did not lift her paw against him, and so he asked why she acted as she did.

She answered, "I love you," but he did not understand, nor did he believe her. He had dealt in falsehoods, and now expected them of others, little thinking that the Mother of All could no more lie than she could cease to exist. They strove in mind against each other, and finally she won. Then she knew that the other powers had used the wrong approach against the Young Tom, trying to use his own creation against him. Instead she dealt with him out of her own nature, which is love so great that it called life into being.

She looked full into his mismatched eyes with the love of her nature, and then he saw as if through her eyes. He saw what he had brought into the worlds, and the pain that his contributions had caused, to her and to others. And he saw, too, that she loved him; not as he had been, nor as he should have been or could have been, but as he was. He could not bear the burden of the fullness of that sight as it filled him. He lay at her feet and grieved, as his sisters had grieved, for the wrongs that he had done, and the imbalance he had caused. He wanted to make reparation, but he did not know what would be sufficient.

Then the Queen did lift her paw: she cuffed him across the ears so hard that he saw stars, but he did not draw back from her. The Queen leaned down and bit him on the back of the neck, and he purred his assent. The Young Tom wanted to give himself, the only thing he had left, to repair what he had done. He breathed out, and closed his eyes, and willed that this death would be the last and greatest, and that with this he would be able to take his creation into himself and out of the worlds. He waited for the bite that would break his neck, but it did not come.

The bite did not come. Instead, he felt himself lifted tenderly by the scruff and carried like a kitten. He did not know how long she carried him, but he felt himself grow cold and wet, as if she carried him through a river. When she put him down, he was wet all over, but she was dry. When he looked around, with his mismatched eyes, he saw his sisters, and the Old Tom. He did not know what to say to them, but the Queen said, "It is good," and the Old Tom curled up around his wet body, and the Young Tom felt the Old Tom's heat warming him. His sisters sat around them and greeted him joyfully. The Queen lay down on his other side and began to wash his ears like a kitten's, and with her licks, he felt his ragged ears become whole again. She said,

"It is good. You are good. Let this ninth life be a true life, now that you have seen truly."

He looked into her eyes, and he saw there both the darkness and the light, and it reminded him of the moon, which grows dark and light by turns. "Yes," she said, "You came from me, and so there is darkness in me, for all that is, is in me. But there is more than that; all the death you have brought has returned lives to me that have been made new. They live now with me, where they are ever in the light and warmth of the Old Tom. I have resolved them into balance within myself, and your choice will enact that same healing within the worlds. You have chosen anew. You have returned to us, and in this is the healing of all hurts.

"I have laid on you a heavier burden than you thought: you will not die and remove hate and death forever, but rather you will live, and use that life to make all anew, especially what is affected by hate and death. Now will night be a time for rest and growth, and winter a time of preparation for the spring. And death itself will be brought into balance: not a horror, but a transition; not an ending, but a change necessary to preserve the balance of the worlds. You will work in the worlds again, making life out of love, alongside your sisters, and the worlds themselves will rise up and help you. And when the balance has shifted, all will be brought into the ninth life, the truer life, the life which is in the heart of love."

The Shaman Visits the House of Dust

Joseph Murphy

Light gathered from whitecap and cloud
Kept my craft,
From the gatekeeper's sight.

I kept beak beneath snake-shaped gunwales,
Drum still: stern above threshold
As another crossed.

That being drew its last breath
As I swerved past the scribe:
That other's name struck
From a tablet's ever-soft clay.

Silent, mote-sized, I eased my craft
Above souls
Shredding final dreams; circled
Miles-long tables.

The breathless

Chewed lumps of dirt, muddied water

Spilling from their cups.

Words spoken of the dead in jest

Hung from their mouths

A specter tried in vain to restore its portrait.

The scale of its cries stirred my drum's skin:

A patch of keel showed. But it failed

To notice; to toss its

Barbed net.

Breath held, I forced my prow further down;

Crossed the final bridge.

Mooring, I found the flower-scented chamber:

The eldest one hovered

Above a nine-limbed tree.

Gifts were offered; mercy given

When deserved. A line of souls

Bowed in turn, waited.

I had come to seek a cure; put beak
To drum.

The eldest one gestured.

I presented a blade
Hammered from lightning bolt shards; an arrow
Shaped from white-hot coals
Cooled on my tongue.

The eldest one offered me a cedar chest.

As I gazed at the lid it seemed
I could see nothing else:

Even through my thousand-fold hawk's eyes;
Though perched at a height
Greater than I had ever flown.

Even with world-spanning wings
Fully opened,
It dwarfed my plumes.

I couldn't hear my drum; taste,
Though my barbed snake's tongue
Lapped the darkness.

It took the will of all my spirits to lift the lid.

As I began to decipher
Lines cut across its lapis lazuli,
My talons lost hold: I woke
To chanting; dancers circling
The pit where I lie.

I could still see its sky-blue carvings
As I rose to sing:
A map, a way through;
A measure of mercy
For those who must die.

Theseus, Considering the Ball of Thread

Hillary Lyon

to unwind this maze
consciousness uncurls
like a pale flower
greeting the watery light
of the moon

in the shadows
of these dank corridors
I hear the oracles in the air
dropping shards of words
over this terra incognito
of our time -- sowing history
in the valleys -- in the fields
the soldiers of the earth
read the scrolls of invention
crumbling as they pass
from hand to hand -- I grab
at the idea of that ragged parchment

fluttering before me

like a battle flag signaling

humanity's stubborn survival

like the single thread of belief

to pilot us home

Orion: An EcoFable

Rebecca Buchanan

In ancient times, there was a great hunter named Orion who became too proud of his skill. No animal -- not deer or bison or swift-footed hare or quick-winged bird -- could escape his arrows. So great was his fame, so well-known his arrogance, that when he challenged the Maiden of the Wilds to a hunt, she accepted. They set out together through woodlands, through jungles, through forests, each bearing but a single bow and a single arrow. When they came upon a herd of mule deer, the Maiden of the Wilds drew her single arrow and slew an aging buck, long past stud. Orion drew his arrow and chose a doe heavy with unborn fawn, and boasted that he had slain two for her one.

They retrieved their arrows and set out through grasslands, across plains, and through valleys. When they came upon a troop of bison, the Maiden of the Wilds drew her arrow and slew a cow hobbled by hunger. Orion drew his arrow, choosing the largest bull. He boasted that he had killed the strongest for her weakest.

They retrieved their arrows and set off through deserts, over mesas, and through canyons. When they came upon a drove of hare, they each drew their arrow. The Maiden of the Wilds chose a kitten with a crippled leg, while Orion slew a buck who could leap far. He boasted that he had killed a hearty animal to her flawed one.

They retrieved their arrows and set out through swamps, through marshes, and across rivers. When they came to a flush of mallard ducks, Orion drew his arrow immediately and slew a drake as he swam. The Maiden of the Wilds waited until the ducks had taken flight, and brought down a hen with her single arrow. Orion boasted that his was the better means, as it assured him a kill.

The Maiden of the Wilds turned to Orion then and warned him: "Your pride blinds you, hunter, to how you offend Earth Mother. You kill the pregnant, the strong, the quick, and the helpless. How, then, are the children of Earth Mother to remain strong and quick and grow in numbers if you hunt them so?"

At her words, Orion laughed and proclaimed, "If the children of Earth Mother are weak and helpless and their numbers dwindle, it is by their fault and hers, not my own."

The Maiden of the Wilds put away her single arrow and warned him once again, "Take care of your words, hunter, for even the smallest and weakest of Earth Mother's children is more noble than you."

Orion laughed again at her words and sat down to enjoy the fruits of his hunt. He soon grew tired from his exertions, and the feast, and fell asleep. In the cool of the night, a tiny scorpion crawled out of its hiding place and across Orion's leg. Awakening, the hunter spied the arthropod and lunged to kill it. The scorpion scuttled away, making for the safety of its hiding place once more, but the hunter cornered it. The scorpion turned to defend itself, and, as the hunter brought his foot down, it sank its stinger deep into his ankle. Only then, as the poison ran through his veins, through his heart, through his brain, did Orion realize his folly and the wisdom of the Maiden's words.

"Forgive me, Earth Mother, for the harm I have done your children, for the strong and the quick and the young that I have taken."

And Orion died.

When the Maiden of the Wilds learned of his death, she took seven bright stones of Earth Mother and cast them into the air. Sky Father took the stones and made the shape of Orion in the night, in testament to his folly and his wisdom, gained too late.

Hadrian in Hyperborea:
The Enigma of the Emperor's Wanderings
P. Sufenas Virius Lupus

Though he knew Sabina Augusta would never have been unfaithful to him, Hadrian sent away Gaius Suetonius Tranquillus, his *ab epistulis*, when a court intrigue suggested that he had an affair with the Empress. Suetonius had been impudent, and far too arrogant for a mere equestrian; and yet, he had a way with words that Hadrian admired, and he suspected that had he not been dismissed, he would have put the particular color of the sunset over Britannia's northern reaches to vibrant words for the readers of posterity. As it was, Hadrian would have to simply keep the memory of the sunset for himself, as none of his hunting companions seemed to care one way or another about it, nor even to have noticed its majesty.

A long day at hunting was coming to a close, and the horses and hounds were weary, though Hadrian was full of vigor. He lamented that his best horse, Borysthenes, had died in Gaul before crossing to Britannia several months prior. Sometimes, he regretted his own decisions, as with Suetonius; and sometimes, he regretted that the gods had not given him more time with those he loved best. Plotina and Matidia were now not only *Augustae*, but *Divae*, and with them nearly all of the family that he ever knew -- his mother and father, his adoptive father Divus Traianus, and the *Divus'* sister Diva Marciana -- had passed on to the afterlife and into the company of the gods. With only his sister Paulina, and his wet-nurse Germana -- a slave, but as close to him as any member of his family ever had been -- among the living, and Sabina not likely to produce an heir, Hadrian tried to take comfort in the chase and forget his many troubles. The Judeans were quiet for the moment; the Parthians no longer a threat; the Britons could resume rioting at any point … even the Calydonian and Erymanthian boars together as the targets of their hunt would have been tame by comparison to any of those nations. But, though a boar was certainly the quarry of the day, no man among them had seen even a bristle of it speeding by; the tracks were plain, its rutting sounds clear and distinct, and the scent hounds were on alert at all times, but it seemed to elude them at every turn.

It was not until the final rays of the sun set Britannia's skies aflame that Hadrian saw it, plain as Trajan's aspect, in the distance: not only a boar of great size, but a *white* boar. Such a beast would make the menagerie of the greatest kings of the east pale in comparison if taken alive, and would put the reputation of the greatest hunters of legend to shame if slain. There was no question: the hunt must continue.

With only three of his men vigorous enough to continue with him, Hadrian rode hard in pursuit, through fields and forests, across meadows and hills. The boar turned and stopped to face them just before a river, as if taunting and tempting them on purpose, and then rushed over a narrow and shallow ford. Hadrian felt as if something was strange about this boar, and when he came to the river's banks, he looked for further signs of it on the other side, and saw nothing. The humming in his ears was no longer the pulse of his heart's blood in excitement: it was as if the string of a kithara was vibrating longer than any musician had been able to make such an instrument hum, to the point that Pythagoras himself would have not had words or numbers to describe it. The dimming light of the day seemed for a moment to waver, and to even brighten briefly. And, for some strange reason, a smell of sweetness was heavy in the air, as if the smoke from the incense of a thousand temples was wafting on the breeze. In his brief reverie, he thought he could taste the meat of the white boar, already roasted and covered in honey, upon his tongue as he paused.

Hadrian spurred on his horse, and they crossed the ford where the boar had been moments before.

When he reached the other side of the river, there was no question: there was music in the air, of an innumerable consort of kithara and barbita and lyre, of chime and cymbal and flutes of every length and width and wood in the forest and of every reed of the marsh, of bagpipe and horn and drum, and bells from the size of fingernails up to the size of wagons. It was no longer dusk -- it was as bright as noon in the Syrian desert on a summer day. And if the sweet smell of incense was heavy before, now it was as if the atmosphere itself was sublimated ambrosia that nourished with its every inhalation. Hadrian dismounted, took the reins of his horse Bukephalos in his hands, and looked back across the river. The sight of his three men approaching on horse was like a dream fading into memory from his earliest childhood, all color drained from it, all sounds as they called to him like the elongated moment before hitting the sand in the palaestra after a blow to the head in the *pankration*.

He saw them dismount, call to him, raise their arms and wave their hands, and walk with their horses across the shallow, narrow ford. As they stood in the small amount of water, men in armor evaporated and washed away like chalk drawings in a sudden downpour. The horses were left without riders, roaming free on the other side of the river.

"Bukephalos, I fear we are no longer in Britannia."

I have no doubt you are correct, Imperator.

The horse's lips did not move, nor did its tongue articulate a sound, but the words it spoke were as clear as the waters of Lake Nemi to the Emperor, and its eyes reflected a rational soul to Hadrian's dumbfounded gaze.

"None shall come here!"

A shout from behind him startled the Emperor. He turned to see a beautiful young man a head taller than him, holding a bronze spear and a shield of alder-wood. A crown of alder leaves was on his head, and besides a bronze torc around his neck and a sword belt with sheathed sword at his waist, the only thing covering the man's body was red paint in jagged stripes.

"Unless you are a poet bringing praise, a craftsman bearing skills, or a crowned king amongst the tribes, none shall come here without doing battle with me!"

Hadrian heard what sounded like his own voice in his ear, feeding him words that would not have been his own under any other circumstance, which he repeated aloud to his challenger.

"I am a poet amongst the Greeks, an artist amongst the Romans, and the Emperor over the lands surrounding the Mediterranean Sea -- we have not had kings since Tarquinus Superbus was driven from the Eternal City of Seven Hills. And if it is the plying of warrior feats at which you wish to be this day, I can meet you with sword or with spear, with shield-tricks and with javelin's sting, or even with the might of my own two arms against your body and whatever strength may be in it."

"Good is your response, stranger, and good shall your welcome be, if you deserve it, between me and the gods! From whence have you come?"

"From near and from far -- an hour's journey south is my men's camp, but I have come from Hispania, via Parthia and Palmyra and Paphlagonia, Greece and Germania and Gaul, the Danube and Dacia and Dalmatia, and the city of Rome itself."

"Far have you traveled, and far-famed is your repute: you are Hadrian, the Emperor of the Romans. How have you found the Isle of the Mighty?"

"I have found it sparse and barbaric and dangerous, and I have found it splendid and beautiful and deserving of praise."

"Your words are pleasing, and your welcome will be without grudge or lack of hospitality! I shall call upon my companion to provide you your lodging for the night, and on the morrow you will see what wonders there are in this land."

"What is your name?"

"In your language, it cannot be spoken; but, in future times I will be worshipped by your people under a name that is called 'The Red God.'"

"Is your nature human, or divine?"

"Though human thought reckons these two states as two separate natures, in reality they are closer than is often realized. The humans of one age are the gods of the next, and the gods of two ages passed are the elder powers of their descendants. I was of the Golden Age before the fall of Kronos, to a Greek's reckoning. We live, we die, we are reborn and pass from form to form; and for this, we are sometimes called gods by the men who live upon the earth at present."

"I …"

His own voice in his ears was silent as Angerona. For the first time in his life, Hadrian did not have a response. His challenger lowered his spear and shield, and began to laugh.

"A golden tongue spoke moments ago, and now the golden tongue has become a knotted golden torc! No matter -- there will be much time to discuss and debate and deliberate over future words and actions and plans in the days to come. Now, you must attend our feast, and be welcomed by your host."

As the red-painted naked man-god lead Hadrian and Bukephalos toward a circular house, the sound of the kithara-string in eternal humming seemed to get louder and louder. As they entered the house, with gilded wooden walls and with swans' feathers as roof thatch, a beautiful man in a green mantle fastened with a brooch of amber sat in the middle of the room playing a strange stringed instrument nearly his own height, triangular in shape, and with more strings upon it than three kitharas, and he plucked the strings without a plectrum. It appeared that the drone that Hadrian heard since he stood on the other side of the river was coming from the longest strings on this instrument, played by this second man-god of Britannia.

"Maponos, this is Hadrian, Emperor of the Romans."

Though he took his fingers away from the instrument, the song continued, albeit diminished in volume. "The Roman Emperor? Here? It is an honor to receive you, my lord!"

Hadrian did not feel comfortable being addressed in such a manner by someone so clearly above him in every sense.

"Even absent the Muses, I would recognize you anywhere: you are Apollon Kitharoidos!"

The two man-gods laughed.

"It is an easy mistake to make. No, I am not Apollon, I am Maponos, as my colleague said. But Apollon is not a stranger to our country -- in fact, he comes to these parts every wintertide."

It all suddenly made sense. Antimachus of Colophon had said that the land of Hyperborea was beyond the Alps, and thus was in the land of the Keltoi and the Galli and the Germans. He had admired the poet's work for years in his youth, and though he thought his stories of the location of the great land of eternal sun to the North were only fables, Hadrian had secretly wished they were true when first he crossed the Alps and came to the *limes* in the German provinces. Hekateos of Abdera had also long suggested that Britannia was Hyperborea. Indeed, in Britannia's north, it seemed Hadrian was in Hyperborea, where a day is a thousand years long, and neither feet nor ships would lead one to its road, as Pindar had written.

For the evening, and three more following it, Hadrian spent time with Maponos, hearing of the history of Hyperborea and its inhabitants, their customs and their crafts, their lives and their loves. The flesh of a great white boar was their food each day, which did not diminish no matter how much had been eaten; and fragrant apples red-gold in hue and kraters of mead were their tastes' delectation.

At what he felt was the noon hour of the third day, he looked out the door of Maponos' house, and saw for the first time the peaks of the Rhipean Mountains, which seemed to be to the south, and to reach so high that nothing beyond them was visible -- not sky nor clouds nor stars. He learned from Maponos that Hyperborea was not the land of Britannia itself, nor Hibernia, nor even Thule or the Isles of Kronos beyond these, of which he had heard tales when he was in Britannia, and amongst the Dacians and Thracians during his wars against them under Trajan. However, as Maponos related to him, in the northern reaches of Britannia, and some parts of its west and south, there were places where a crossing to Hyperborea could be made, often with little notice for those making the crossing. It was this ease of access to divine realms that made the Britons so ferocious and fearless of death. If the peoples of Rome and Greece and the rest of Europa knew that it was so easy to access the lands where the gods themselves spent their holidays, Britannia might be overrun by settlers of every rank and repute clamoring for a place amongst the godly hosts. Hadrian was fortunate, and he knew it, and knew that such knowledge could not be squandered.

As the fourth day dawned, Maponos at last told Hadrian that he had been given leave to take him to the Temple of Apollon at the heart of Hyperborea's lands, where the three brothers, the Boreades, were giant kings who held court in absence of the god, and who were titanic priests in the god's presence. Maponos and three Hyperborean nymphs took Hadrian to a pond in the nearby woods, where they all bathed together. The cleansing of Hadrian after hunt and travels was a welcome affair, but the Hyperboreans had little but the sweetness of idle heat sweat, which for all that still had the fragrance of pine and juniper, to wash away with clean clear water that smelled of roses. The nymphs clad their shoulders in cloths of spun gold, translucent in the rays of Hyperborea's never-dimming sun, while Maponos fastened on his green mantle once again. They wore no clothing around their lower bodies, for in Hyperborea, hiding beauty was considered a crime as grave as murder amongst humans. Recognizing that he was not of their world, and would need to be marked as such, Hadrian was given a breastplate of bronze emblazoned with Medusa's visage to wear over his purple tunic.

Joined by the man-god painted in red jagged stripes, Maponos, Hadrian, and the three nymphs went to the north and in what seemed like hours that were only moments, and over distances that in truth were provinces and continents but which passed under the gentle lights of the Hyperborean sun like a pleasant afternoon at rest in Latium, they came to the crystalline columns of the great circular temple of Apollon, as tall as if the Capitoline Hill of Rome sat atop the Akropolis of Athens at the crest of Arkadia's Mt. Lykaion. To merely state that the Emperor was in awe would make Themis dull her sword.

The Three Boreades emerged from their temple, each of them half again as tall as Maponos and the red man-god, and each identical to the other, with hair of pure white after their mother Khione, and with the strength of fifty horses in each of their limbs. Though no winds gentle nor fierce blew upon the plains of Hyperborea, the Three Boreades seemed as if their long and radiant hair was constantly being tossed about by the invisible hands of Zephyros. They embraced Hadrian in welcome, and each was cold to the touch like ice eternally unmelting.

"Three Priests, Three Kings, Three Gods of Skill, we have brought you the Emperor of the Romans, Publius Aelius Hadrianus."

"Well have we known you would come, and well met is your arrival," the Three Boreades said in unison. "What does the Sovereign of the World wish of the Three Kings of Hyperborea?"

Hadrian had known they would make their visit for days, and had rehearsed his response a thousand times in his thoughts. Still, the sound of his words stated before he could speak them hung in his ears along with the endless drone of Maponos' unplucked strings.

"I wish to have knowledge from the god Apollon."

"Knowledge comes at a price, Emperor. Are you willing to pay that price?"

"I am."

But, what would that price be? Would he lose a single eye, a tooth, or a decade of his life? Would he become blind, like Tiresias, or would he fill with despair of the world after seeing such splendor while still mortal? He knew there were many possibilities, and he spoke of all of them with Maponos over the last few days, but what his fate would be and what the price of his knowledge would become, he could not fathom, and was not yet told.

"Very well. Come to the doors of the temple and make your sacrifice."

Wait -- he had not prepared a sacrifice! He thought himself foolish and neglectful, and filled with the greatest hubris and arrogance imaginable, to expect such knowledge to come even at whatever cost would be asked of him, without first giving an honorable and appropriate sacrifice to the god.

As he approached the doors of the temple, trembling and expecting that he might be turned away in shame, he saw the red god-man and another man -- familiar, and yet unknown to him -- standing near to the doors with the great white boar, alive before them, and entirely tame.

Before the temple's altar, he asked the boar if it was willing to be his sacrifice to the god, and the boar answered with its own voice gladly and in the affirmative.

With a knife given from the red god-man, and the white boar itself stretching its neck, Hadrian slew the boar and let its blood pour into several offering bowls of lapis lazuli and gold, which was then offered in the blue-gold flames on the altar before the temple doors. The Three Boreades opened the doors of the temple and entered, and closed the doors again; within, Hadrian could see a statue of Apollon that must have been taller than the Kolossos at

Rhodes, and all of amber, a vision cut short when the priest-kings slammed the doors to his profane eyes.

While the Three Boreades communed with the god, the entire temple seemed to be engulfed in blue-gold flames, and yet not a single part of it was diminished or damaged from the conflagration.

After a time which was hours that seemed like seconds, and the Hyperborean sun stayed fixed in the sky as if fastened to the firmament with a divine nail of unimaginable height, the unquenchable fires upon the temple subsided, and the Three Boreades returned.

"The Great God Apollon is not in Hyperborea now; his presence is unseen, but potent, in Delphi with his oracle there, for it is the summer months in your world. However, we are priests and oracles in this place, in which no riddling words nor enigmatic responses accompany the wisdom and the dictates of the Great God. Every question you have will be answered, even though you will not ask them with the breath of your thoughts. Hear now the words of the Great God."

And for the first time, the Three Boreades did not speak in unison, but instead began dancing a circle around Hadrian, speaking in turn.

"Our world withdraws from yours faster each year,
Though for this mortals know not, nor shed a tear …"
"But the ties are not broken, the bridges still strong,
And will remain so for a century long …"

"But while borders still blur, protection is needed,
Thus with bricks and with trenches the isle
will be seeded ..."

"A day is a thousand years for this land,
And thus sixty years' time for a life is grand ..."

"Thus, more than two hundred thousand years in age
Is a Hyperborean sixty-year-old sage ..."

"And with such a life in golden days and no night
A sage welcomes death without sadness nor spite ..."

"Falling to waves and drowning in sea,
From this fate our people do not flee ..."

"To return to Nyx's sheltering dark
and rekindle again the divine spark ..."

"But remember, you are human, and it is not meet
For you at sixty to such actions repeat ..."

"You will live longer than sixty, your horoscope states,
Though sadness and loss lies in the fates ..."

"Of those close to you and of whom you will love;
Do not fear when a drowning makes stars shine above ..."

"For the gods in their goodness will welcome the one
For whom the red garlands of lotus are won ..."

"But now, to the matter of prices to pay
For the words of prediction the God gives this day …"

"The giving of offerings to the nymphs of old
On Delos' isle, from Hyperborea's fold …"

"Has been broken, for Arimaspi are blind,
And Issedones have been routed in kind …"

"Thus to Dodona our gifts cannot pass:
Now you must be the one who will amass …"

"Our gifts, packed in straw, and carry them east
To provide for our nymph heroines' feast …"

"When the gifts come to you, on three occasions,
You must not hesitate to make vacations …"

"And hie to Hellas, and pass them to another
Who'll convey them to shrine of Artemis' brother …"

"But one last blessing will be given to you
So that this task you have yet to do …"

"May take place with ease, despite failing limbs
As life in the flesh wanes, waxes, and dims …"

"For your health to the age of sixty-two
Apollon's *paean* will be performed for you."

And as the import of these verses had yet to dawn on Hadrian, a rush of wings was soon heard on the air, and a flock of swans in the hundreds of thousands descended on the vicinity of the temple of Apollon in Hyperborea. In unison, they sang a song so surpassing in beauty that Hadrian fell to his knees and wept and trembled as its chords rang out. He could feel the blood seething within him, not in pain or in stress, but in effervescence and refreshment, as his flesh was regenerated and healed of his growing complaints of age, disease, and the life of a legionary commander in several wars under Trajan. His senses scrambled and he began to endure waves of vertigo as his body's rhythms were rewritten to make his health improve.

In what fleeting moments of consciousness he had within him in his Hyperborean sojourn remained, he saw that the other man that stood with the white boar as sacrifice was not a man, nor a god-man like the others, nor a giant nor indeed a very god, but instead his horse Bukephalos who had taken on a human shape for a few moments -- or was it days or even years? -- while they remained in the land of the endless sun. The red god-man and Maponos and the three nymphs helped to convey Hadrian and Bukephalos back to Britannia, and in doing so they took the form of wolves which moved faster than the steeds of Boreas himself in accompanying them.

Hadrian awoke amongst his men and their horses -- the men who had evaporated in the river -- with his brazen breastplate and the carcass of the great white boar, to the north near his encampment in the northern reaches of Britannia. They had only been waiting for a few moments when he returned across the river with the boar on his shoulders -- though still impressive, it was much smaller than it had been in Hyperborea -- in a near Bacchic-like fury, bloodied and singing a song that seared itself into their minds for the remainder of their days. Upon returning to the southern side of the river, he collapsed in exhaustion, and had slept for a few hours before he awoke, somewhat dazed but delighted, and still singing the song.

Two days after returning to his men, he gave a speech on his plans for a wall, fortified on the south side with a trench, that would stretch across the neck of the isle of Britannia's north. He said it was to delineate the limits of the Empire, to regulate trade, and to more easily repel invasions from the Caledonian tribes and to divide them from their more southerly kinsmen. This was all done across a great northern river, at a new bridge that Hadrian had built, forbidding ships and ferries to cross its currents. He named the place where the bridge was built Pons Aelius.

In the coming months, he was struck with a great desire to go to Greece after inspecting the Legions in Africa. He did not indicate any plans to do so before, but his urgency was met with compliance by the entire court.

He instructed that many buildings at his Villa in Tibur, his mausoleum near the Vatican Hill, and a new temple in Rome all be made in circular patterns, which was most unusual for Greek and Roman buildings.

Six years later, after touring much of the Empire, again Hadrian decided to head east, and took with him his wife Sabina and his young lover, Antinous. In two years, Antinous would be dead from drowning in the Nile.

After returning from his eastern sojourns, trouble erupted again in Judea. At long last, Hadrian joined his legions there, via Greece, after suddenly deciding to stop there along the way once more.

He died at the age of sixty-two, having outlived the rest of his family, his wife, and his lover, with only his wet-nurse surviving him.

He spoke of Hyperborea once, to his second adopted son Antoninus, just before his death. Antoninus did not believe his feverish ravings on his deathbed; but, he ordered a wall to be built north of Hadrian's Wall all the same….

Navigatio Gaii Suetonii Paullini ex Britannia ad Ogygia et Insulas Saturni

P. Sufenas Virius Lupus

Six years and six months were they wandering in the ocean...

I.

There was a governor of Britannia, Gaius Suetonius Paullinus by name. He had been a praetor, and when he was sent as a legionary legate to Mauretania to suppress a rebellion, he crossed the Atlas Mountains and explored the interior of Africa. There he came into contact with the tribes of the Blemmyae, whose faces are in their chests since they lack heads, and the Pygmies, who are in constant warfare with the flocks of cranes in their land, and the tribes of the Gymnosophists who had come from India, and with Troglodytes and Ethiopians and Nubians and with other races, as told elsewhere.

When Paullinus was sent to Britannia, he pursued the suppression of the tribes of Britons on the west of the island. Eventually, he came to assault the stronghold of the druids on the isle of Mona. The battle was ferocious, but he and his men managed to put the druids to flight and to the sword and to drowning themselves in the sea for fear of the Romans. But, their victory was not without consequence, for before the death of the last druid on the isle, a curse was laid upon Paullinus and his men, that they would venture forth from the isle to return to Britannia, but would not be able to do so for the length of six years and six months. Paullinus, upon hearing this, thought nothing of it, for the distance between Mona and Britannia's mainland was not far -- in fact, one could be seen from the shores of the other.

Paullinus and his officers set out in their boat, and a mist soon enveloped them. They steered toward where the mainland of Britannia should have been, but after a day, and two, and three, they did not reach it. On the dawn of the fourth day, they saw a man riding on horseback, but his horse trod upon the waves as if they were sods of earth.

"Who are you, and how have you come to be in such a state?" Paullinus asked the rider.

"I am a Thracian of the region of Sardica, and was in the Roman army. Longinus son of Sdapezematygus is my name."

"How have you come to be here, Longinus?"

"I have been deceased for many years, but my soul lives on in these regions. My bodily remains are under the earth in Camulodunum, but they will not remain so for long, for the tribe of the Iceni are about to attack that fort, and lay waste to the rest of the cities of Britannia."

"How have you come to know this?"

"Knowledge is not at its ceasing simply because death has occurred. You will find knowledge and the power to accomplish the defeat of the Iceni if you listen carefully to my instructions. There are many islands of wonder to the west of here, and you will make the rounds of them for six years and six months before returning to Britannia; however, as long as you never set foot on one of those islands for more than four days before returning to your boat, these six years and six months will pass for you like moments once you return to Britannia. The first island is five days' sail west of here."

The Romans under Paullinus therefore set their sails and their oars to the direction of Favonius' wind.

II.

After sailing for five days, they came to a small island in the sea. The shores seemed to be made of gold, and there were figures visible on the shore. As they neared the island, some of Paullinus' men scrambled off the boat and came ashore, taking large nuggets of gold in their hands and rejoicing at their fortune. But, it was worse for them, because soon the figures visible on the shore came closer, and proved to be very large ants who guarded the gold. The ants seized the soldiers in their powerful mouth-claws, and soon they were torn limb from limb for their greed. The Romans under Paullinus had no choice but to pass onwards again.

III.

After three days of sailing further, they came to a small island that was high in the middle, but which had terraces around it leading up to its height. At the center of the isle was a circle of trees, and there were birds in every tree. Paullinus and his men explored the island, and found nothing in it that was threatening or dangerous, and they ate their fill of the birds from the trees. They took more birds for the journey, and went on their way once again.

IV.

They were at sea for three more days, until they came to an island that was broad before them. The shores of the island were vast in sand dunes, and from behind one of the dunes a strange creature appeared. It had the body of a horse, but the feet of a hunting hound. The creature bayed and rutted at seeing them, for it seemed to be in great joy at their coming; but, the crew of Paullinus' ship, fearful of such a beast, began to row away from the island. The beast then began to rage and warp itself, and in doing so it stirred up the sand and pelted the crew with pebbles. The crew feared they would not be able to escape from it, but a prevailing wind soon carried their boat elsewhere.

V.

The following day, they came to a great island in the sea that was broad, flat, and fair. They came ashore, and after walking about for a short while, they found what looked like the hoof-print of a horse, but it was as large as the sail of their ship. They heard a great cry of a multitude in the distance, and in fear, they fled to their ship and sailed around the edges of the island. Behold, they saw upon the island an army of centaurs, their forms like moving mountains upon the ground, their hair shaggy on their bodies like pine boughs, and their manner and their activities to be racing around in circles as if it was the games of the Megalensia. The Romans under Paullinus were glad that they had fled to their boat, so that they would not be trampled underfoot by these gigantic beasts.

VI.

After a week of sailing further, they came to a great island with a large hall in its center. An ingenious aqueduct was built from the shore of the sea to the side of the hall, such that a stream flowed down from the hall and into the sea, but salmon in great numbers swam up the stream of the aqueduct and directly into the house with great leaps as the sun shimmered off their backs in rainbow hues. When the Romans under Paullinus reached the hall, they found a bed for each of them in the hall, and a plate with a juicy salmon upon it, and a krater full of fine wine upon the table for each of them. They gave thanks to Jupiter Optimus Maximus and Neptune for their fortune, and sat and had their fill of food and wine, and slept soundly for the night, and returned to the sea once more.

VII.

The length of their journey from that island was extended, and with great hunger and fear of starvation, they came to another island enclosed all around with woods. They could not reach the island itself, but instead Paullinus could only hold onto a branch from one of the trees that extended its boughs over the sea. The branch broke off, and though they sailed around the island for three more days, they could not reach a spot to land. On the third day, three apples were found to have grown on the end of the bough in Paullinus' hand, which he had never set down since the time he pulled it from the bough. They gave thanks to Pomona, and each of those apples was large enough to sustain the whole crew for forty days.

VIII.

They came to an island that was surrounded by a low stone wall, which made it difficult to land. However, soon a strange beast came from the interior of the island, and began to do feats in the air above the island. It appeared at first to be a gryphon, with the head and wings of an eagle but the body of a lion, and in this wise it made loops through the air above the wall. Then, it straightened its body out, and its haunches became those of a bull and its head that of a woman, who sang in piercing tones that caused the soldiers' swords to hum in their sheaths. Then its tail became a serpent and its head and foreparts were that of a goat, and it began to bleat and butt its horns agains the stone wall. A shower of stones flew over the sea and struck the shields of the Romans, and many stones remained lodged in their shields thereafter. In hopelessness, the Romans under Paullinus retreated from the island.

IX.

After endless days of travel upon the wide sea, they came to another island with four horses upon it. The names of those horses were Podagrus, Lampion, Xanthus, and Deinus. The four horses ran about the island chasing each other, and when they would come close to another, they would take a bite of the other's flesh, which sent forth a stream of blood that was hot and steaming, but which would soon be staunched if the wounded horse could take a bit of another. In eternal strife and contention were these horses unless they could find a further source of meat upon which to slake their hunger. The Romans under Paullinus, in great despair, left the vicinity of the island where the mares of Diomedes had been imprisoned after Hercules had stolen them.

X.

They came to a further island in the sea, which had this quality: it stood on four pillars. Paullinus knew this island was called Ortygia, and it had been the birthplace of the children of Latona, Apollo and Diana. Upon the shore of the island they saw three nymphs of the lands beyond Aquilon. The Romans under Paullinus asked if they might climb up to the island, but the nymphs forbade it, for it was a sacred island on account of the goddess and god who had been born there. (They said the island was also called Emania.) However, the nymphs lowered down to them a flask of sweet water, which satisfied their hunger and thirst for months to come.

XI.

After another month of travel, they came to two islands lying close to one another. On the first island, there was a bronze wall built down the center of it, and there were white sheep on one side of it and black sheep on the other. When a white sheep would jump from one side to the other, it would become black; and when a black sheep would jump from one side to the other, it would become white. Though some Roman soldiers wished to test this island's peculiarities on themselves, Paullinus forbade it.

On the second island, there was a gigantic herdsman sitting beneath a tree, who only had one eye. This eye had a strange quality as well, for though it was at all times open, there was no sight in it. The men under Paullinus tried to inquire of the herdsman what advice he might have, or how he might come to trade them for some of his flock, but the herdsman only replied "I hear NO ONE."

Paullinus soon spotted Longinus, the Thracian rider, coming towards them once again. "I recall," the Thracian said, "that this island was home to the race of the Arimaspi, of whom yonder herdsman is one. But none have come here since the time of Aristeas of Proconnesus." Paullinus asked if the herdsman was the same son of Poseidon that Ulysses had encountered in his wanderings, but the Thracian replied, "Only the gods know if that is true."

XII.

When they had sailed further such that weariness and exhaustion and the nymphs' gift was in its dregs, they saw another island known as Ogygia. On that island, in a fortress made of crystal, dwelt the nymph Calypso, daughter of Atlas, who spent her days weaving upon a golden loom with a golden shuttle. Calypso made the Romans under Paullinus welcome, and bade them to stay with her for three days. In that time, they had their fill of good food and sweet drink, and did not fret nor fear for a moment on account of Calypso's soothing singing voice. On the third day, the crew asked if Paullinus would be a suitable mate for Calypso, but she replied, "There is only one who would have been a suitable mate for me, and he has gone back to Ithaca -- Ulysses the son of Laertes was his name." With that, she asked the crew to depart. When they reached their ship, the crewman who was left behind on it was dead, for though they had only been gone for three days, to the crewman who never set foot on the island of Ogygia, it has been as more than a year.

XIII.

An island belching black smoke soon appeared to the Romans under Paullinus. The smoke was caused from a great fiery forge that was built underneath a tall black mountain. A cleft was in the mountain's side, in the shape of a gigantic man. A goddess came to the shore of the island to speak with the Romans.

"What island is this?"

"It is the isle of Lemnos."

"But is not the isle of Lemnos in the Aegean Sea?"

"There is an island of Lemnos there, but it is not this one; nor is the Delos of the Aegean the Delos you have visited, nor the Ogygia the isle of the Syracusans."

"Who are you?"

"I am Thetis, the mother of Achilleus."

"Who dwells on this island?"

"Who else but the god Vulcan, working at his forge?"

Not accustomed to dealing with the likes of the immortal races, Paullinus and his men soon retreated from the isle of Lemnos and troubled the goddess Thetis no more with their questions.

XIV.

After a few more days of sailing, they came to a great silver pillar in the ocean, with four sides, and words in every language inscribed upon its four faces. A great net of silver strands, with crystals suspended from its junctions, stretched into the sea from the top of the pillar, which they could not see. They tried to sail to where the edge of the net touched the sea, but would become lost. They came to the base of the pillar, and heard a voice from the top of it speaking to them. "You have come near to the end of your journey -- sail to the north of here, and you will come to the isle of the blessed that you seek."

XV.

When the stores of their food and water were nearly exhausted, they came to a bright isle in the sea, over which no storms poured nor did clouds obscure the sun. They landed easily, and found great companies of people upon that island. At the center of the island was a great throne upon which was a gigantic old man, clothed only in his beard and long hair.

Upon the island, the Romans under Paullinus met many heroes of legend, including Achilleus, Helen, and others whose names are known and praised throughout the nations of humankind.

The great bearded giant at the center of the island was Saturn, who ruled over the golden age of humanity, and likewise remained in such a state on this island.

The great companies around Saturn were the heroes and virtuous people, who came to serve a term in honor of Saturn the length of seven years before passing on to Elysium and into the celestial realms.

The inhabitants of that island told Paullinus that it was called Brasilia, and though they would be able to stay for a short while, they would not be able to stay for the seven years, for they had to return to their own lands and to the island of Britannia.

The Romans under Paullinus graciously accepted the hospitality of the people of Brasilia, the heroes of the golden age, and praised Saturn for his hospitality. With Agamemnon and the other heroes of the Trojan War, Paullinus spoke of military strategy and tactics, and became well informed on how to proceed in the future when he would face the Iceni revolt.

It was not known how much time had passed since they came to that island.

XVI.

They came to one final island before returning to Britannia. The island was just off the coast of Brasilia, and boasted great fields of flowers: asphodel and narcissus and lotuses.

There were people there eating the lotus flowers in particular.

The crew of Romans under Paullinus came ashore and took some of the lotus flowers and ate them. Soon, they were seized with a lethargy and an exhaustion, and laid down to sleep.

From a distance, they heard the voice of Saturn speaking to them: "Those who have eaten of the lotus flowers will no more awaken as living mortals; they may be born again on the earth in the future, but will have forgotten their lives that came before. Do not make the same mistake as them in drinking from the spring of Lethe!"

XVII.

Soon enough, the crew of Romans under Paullinus reached the shores of Britannia, opposite the isle of Mona. They set down upon the shore, and found that they had not been missed by their brethren back on the mainland. They proceeded to Londinium, and eventually faced the Iceni in great numbers under their queen, Boudicca, and defeated her. Nothing was said of their journeys in the western expanses of ocean, and the many islands they visited.

XVIII.

When Paullinus was no longer governor of Britannia, he became a consul in Rome. When his consulship was finished, he went to Athens, where he met a student of Ammonius from the Academy named Lucius Mestrius Plutarchus, to whom he told of his adventures in the western ocean and the wondrous islands they visited. But Plutarchus dismissed his tales as so much barbarian nonsense, and thought little of it for most of the remainder of his life.

Our Contributors

Scathe meic Beorh is a mythologian and writer who lives with his wife Ember on the Atlantic Coast of Florida. He is the author of the mythological studies *Emhain Macha Dark Rain* (RS Press) and *Golgotha* (Punkin House), and the mythological satire *The Pirates of St. Augustine* (Wildside Press).

Elizabeth Bodien lives near Hawk Mountain, Pennsylvania. She taught anthropology until 2007. Her poetry has appeared in *The Litchfield Review*, *The Fourth River*, *US 1 Worksheets*, and *Cimarron Review*, among other publications in the United States, Australia, Canada, India, and Ireland. Her collections include *Plumb Lines* (Plan B Press 2008), *Rough Terrain: Notes of an Undutiful Daughter* (FootHills Publishing 2010), and *Endpapers* (Finishing Line Press 2011).

Rebecca Buchanan is the editor-in-chief of Bibliotheca Alexandrina. She also edits the Pagan literary ezine *Eternal Haunted Summer*, and blogs regularly at *BookMusings: (Re)Discovering Pagan Literature*.

Valentina Cano is a student of classical singing who spends whatever free time she has either reading or writing. She also watches over a veritable army of pets. Her work has appeared in numerous publications and her poetry has been nominated for the Pushcart Prize and Best Of the Web. You can find her here: carabosseslibrary.blogspot.com

Larisa Hunter, the oldest of three girls, spent most of her life on the East Coast of Canada. Although she was raised as a Jehovah's Witness, she was fortunate enough to have very open-minded parents that shared with her a love of history and culture. It was her discovery of Asatru that changed everything. By 2003 Larisa took her oath of profession, taking the name Mist. Under that name she contributed to *Odin's Gift*, a heathen poetry page, and became a member of Asatru Ring Frankfurt. She relinquished Mist later on, preferring to use her given name. Larisa is the gods-woman of Kenaz Kindred, named after the elder futhark rune which symbolizes the torch of knowledge. Kenaz Kindred strives to incorporate the spiritual with the historical in its rites, and to being a welcoming and accepting place for heathens. She has lectured at many heathen and pagan festivals and authored two books, *Fulltrui: Patrons in Asatru* and *Embracing Heathenry*. In 2011, she opened Friggas Loom, a business named in honour of her patron goddess where she creates custom made harrow cloths.

Literata Hurley is a Wiccan priestess and writer. Her work has appeared in several anthologies, including *Mandragora, Unto Herself,* and *Anointed* as well as multiple periodicals. She has presented at Sacred Space conference, Fertile Ground Gathering, and local gatherings in the mid-Atlantic area. She is currently completing her doctoral dissertation in history with the support of her husband and four cats. worksofliterata.org

Kit Koinis was raised in New Mexico, visiting her grandparent's ranch regularly, which gave her the appreciation for the rich culture of the Land of Enchantment. She now resides on the East Coast, spinning stories for everyone around her.

Gerri Leen lives in Northern Virginia and originally hails from Seattle. She has a collection of short stories, *Life Without Crows*, out from Hadley Rille Books, and over fifty stories and poems published in such places as: *She Nailed a Stake Through His Head*, *Sword and Sorceress XXIII*, *Dia de los Muertos*, *Return to Luna*, *Sniplits*, *Triangulation: Dark Glass*, *Sails & Sorcery*, and *Paper Crow*. She also is editing an anthology of speculative fiction and poetry from Hadley Rille Books that will benefit homeless animals. Visit gerrileen.com to see what else she's been up to.

P. Sufenas Virius Lupus is a metagender, and the *Doctor*, *Magistratum*, *Mystagogos*, *Sacerdos*, and one of the founding members of the Ekklesía Antínoou -- a queer, Graeco-Roman-Egyptian syncretist reconstructionist polytheist group dedicated to Antinous, the deified lover of the Roman Emperor Hadrian, and related deities and divine figures -- as well as a contributing member of Neos Alexandria and a practicing Celtic Reconstructionist pagan in the traditions of *gentlidecht* and *filidecht*, as well as Romano-British, Welsh, and Gaulish deity devotions. Lupus is also dedicated to several land spirits around the area of North Puget Sound and its islands. Lupus' work (poetry, fiction, and essays) has appeared in a number of Bibliotheca Alexandrina devotional volumes, as well as Ruby Sara's anthologies *Datura* (2010) and *Mandragora* (2012), Inanna Gabriel and C. Bryan Brown's *Etched Offerings* (2011), Lee Harrington's *Spirit of Desire: Personal Explorations of Sacred Kink* (2010), and Galina Krasskova's *When the Lion Roars* (2011). Lupus has also written several full-length books, including *The Phillupic Hymns* (2008), *The Syncretisms of Antinous* (2010), *Devotio Antinoo: The Doctor's Notes, Volume One* (2011), *All-Soul, All-Body, All-Love, All-Power: A TransMythology* (2012), *A Garland for Polydeukion* (2012), and *A Serpent Path Primer* (2012), with more on the way. Lupus writes the "Queer I Stand" column at Patheos.com's Pagan Portal, the "Gentlidecht" blog at PaganSquare, and also blogs at Aedicula Antinoi (http://aediculaantinoi.wordpress.com/).

Since founding Subsynchronous Press in 2000, **Hillary Lyon** has acted as editor for the print poetry journals, *The Laughing Dog* and *Veil: Journal of Darker Musings*. Author of eighteen chapbooks, her poems, short stories, sketches and photographs have appeared in various publications for the last thirty years.

A seven-time Pushcart-Prize nominee and National Park Artist-in-Residence, **Karla Linn Merrifield** has had more than 300 poems appear in dozens of journals and anthologies. She has nine books to her credit, the newest of which are *Lithic Scatter and Other Poems* (Mercury Heartlink) and *The Ice Decides: Poems of Antarctica* (Finishing Line Press). Forthcoming from Salmon Poetry is *Athabaskan Fractal and Other Poems of the Far North*, and from FootHills Publishing, *Attaining Canopy: Amazon Poems.* Her *Godwit: Poems of Canada* (FootHills) received the 2009 Eiseman Award for Poetry and she recently received the Dr. Sherwin Howard Award for the best poetry published in *Weber - The Contemporary West* in 2012. She is assistant editor and poetry book reviewer for *The Centrifugal Eye (*centrifugaleye.com). Visit her blog, *Vagabond Poet*, at karlalinn.blogspot.com.

Joseph Murphy is a professional editor and writer who lives in Michigan. He has had poetry published in a number of journals, including *The Gray Sparrow*, *The Ann Arbor Review* and *The Sugar House Review*. Murphy is also a poetry editor for an online literary journal, *Halfway Down the Stairs*.

George H. Northrup is President (2006-) of the Fresh Meadows Poets in Queens, NY, a Board member of the Society that selects the Nassau County Poet Laureate, former President of the New York State Psychological Association, and currently on the Council of Representatives that governs the American Psychological Association. Recent publications include *Buddhist Poetry Review, First Literary Review—East, Generations, Long Island Quarterly, Moebius, The New York Times, Performance Poets Association Literary Review,* and *StepAway Magazine.* georgehnorthrup.com/Poetry.html

Juli D. Revezzo has long been in love with writing, a love built by devouring everything from the Arthurian legends, to the works of Michael Moorcock, and the classics and has a soft spot for classic the "Goths" of the 19th century. Her short fiction has been published in *Dark Things II: Cat Crimes*, *The Scribing Ibis*, *Eternal Haunted Summer*, *Twisted Dreams Magazine*, *Luna Station Quarterly,* and *Crossed Genres'* "Posted stories for Haiti relief" project, while her non-fiction has been included in *The Scarlet Letter.* She has also, on occasion, edited the popular e-zine *Nolan's Pop Culture Review.* But her heart lies in the storytelling. She is a member of the Indie Author Network. Her debut novel, *The Artist's Inheritance,* was recently released.

Ruth Sabath Rosenthal is a New York poet, well published in literary journals and poetry anthologies throughout the U.S., as well as Canada, Greece, Israel, India, Romania, and the U.K. In 2006, Ruth's poem "on yet another birthday" was nominated for a Pushcart prize. Ruth has a book of poems, *Facing Home and Beyond* that can be purchased from amazon.com; barnesandnoble.com; or directly from Ruth, via e-mail: ruthspoems(at)aol.com. She also has a poetry book forthcoming titled *little, but by no means small.* For more about Ruth, please feel free to "Google" her and visit websites:

ruthsabathrosenthal.moonfruit.com

pw.org/content/ruth_sabath_rosenthal,

and poetryvlog.com/ruthsabathrosenthal

Rebecca Lynn Scott lives in Seattle with her wife and far too many four-footed mammals. She blogs about weaving, worship, and magic at ariadne.dememe.info.

Szmeralda Shanel, MA is a visual, ritual and performance artist. She is an initiate in the Anderson Feri/Faery tradition and an ordained priestess of Isis/Auset with the Fellowship of Isis and the Temple of Isis. Szmeralda is the founder of The Iseum of Black Isis, an iseum dedicated to Goddess Spirituality and Sacred Arts. She currently lives in Chicago, IL and works as a teaching artist, expressive arts therapist, and a tarot reader. blackisismagic.com

Brenda Kyria Skotas is a High Priestess of the Bloodroot Honey Priestess Tribe, a Pan-Dianic tradition in the SF Bay Area. A dedicated priestess of Hera, she prides herself on holding safe space for others to heal and find their own strength as sovereign women. In practice she is an animist and Hellenic polytheist with a reverent respect for those who have gone before. A practical and fearless witch, Brenda has created her own path from the remnants of personal experience, failure, a love for fairy tale trickery, and the use of her own hands. Fiber arts, cordials, and scavenged tools are an oft seen part of what takes place before her hearth. You can find more of her writing on her blog, smokefromthetemple.wordpress.com.

Craig W. Steele resides in the countryside of northwestern Pennsylvania, where he is a professor of biology at Edinboro University. He writes for the same reasons he reads -- for enjoyment, to understand, and to visit alternate realities. His work has appeared most recently in *Plainsongs, The Lyric, the Aurorean, Stone Path Review, Popular Astronomy, Enhance* and elsewhere.

Kristin Camitta Zimet is Editor of *The Sow's Ear Poetry Review*. She is author of the poetry collection *Take in My Arms the Dark* (1999). Her poems are in many anthologies and journals, including *Poet Lore, Lullwater Review*, and *Salt Hill*. She was recently nominated for a Pushcart Prize and for Best of the Net, and was finalist for the Graybeal-Gowan Prize.

About Bibliotheca Alexandrina

Ptolemy Soter, the first Makedonian ruler of Egypt, established the library at Alexandria to collect all of the world's learning in a single place. His scholars compiled definitive editions of the Classics, translated important foreign texts into Greek, and made monumental strides in science, mathematics, philosophy and literature. By some accounts over a million scrolls were housed in the famed library, and though it has long since perished due to the ravages of war, fire, and human ignorance, the image of this great institution has remained as a powerful inspiration down through the centuries.

To help promote the revival of traditional polytheistic religions we have launched a series of books dedicated to the ancient gods of Greece and Egypt. The library is a collaborative effort drawing on the combined resources of the different elements within the modern Hellenic and Kemetic communities, in the hope that we can come together to praise our gods and share our diverse understandings, experiences and approaches to the divine.

A list of our current and forthcoming titles can be found on the following page. For more information on the Bibliotheca, our submission requirements for upcoming devotionals, or to learn about our organization, please visit us at neosalexandria.org.

Sincerely,
The Editorial Board of the Library of Neos Alexandria

Current Titles

Written in Wine:
    A Devotional Anthology for Dionysos

Dancing God:
    Poetry of Myths and Magicks

Goat Foot God

Longing for Wisdom: The Message of the Maxims

The Phillupic Hymns

Unbound:
    A Devotional Anthology for Artemis

Waters of Life:
    A Devotional Anthology for Isis and Serapis

Bearing Torches:
    A Devotional Anthology for Hekate

Queen of the Great Below:
    An Anthology in Honor of Ereshkigal

From Cave to Sky:
    A Devotional Anthology in Honor of Zeus

Out of Arcadia:
> *A Devotional Anthology for Pan*

Anointed:
> *A Devotional Anthology for the Deities of the Near and Middle East*

The Scribing Ibis:
> *An Anthology of Pagan Fiction in Honor of Thoth*

Queen of the Sacred Way:
> *A Devotional Anthology in Honor of Persephone*

Unto Herself:
> *A Devotional Anthology for Independent Goddesses*

The Shining Cities:
> *An Anthology of Pagan Science Fiction*

Guardian of the Road:
> *A Devotional Anthology in Honor of Hermes*

Harnessing Fire:
> *A Devotional Anthology in Honor of Hephaestus*

Beyond the Pillars:
> *An Anthology of Pagan Fantasy*

Queen of Olympos:

A Devotional Anthology for Hera and Iuno

A Mantle of Stars:
A Devotional Anthology in
Honor of the Queen of Heaven

Forthcoming Titles

Potnia:
>*An Anthology in Honor of Demeter*

By Blood, Bone, and Blade:
>*A Tribute to the Morrigan*

The Queen of the Sky Who Rules Over All the Gods:
>*A Devotional Anthology in Honor of Bast*

Daughter of the Sun:
>*A Devotional Anthology in Honor of Sekhmet*

Seasons of Grace:
>*A Devotional in Honor of the Muses, the Charites, and the Horae*

From the Roaring Deep:
>*A Devotional for Poseidon and the Spirits of the Sea*

Shield of Wisdom:
>*A Devotional Anthology in Honor of Athena*

Megaloi Theoi:
>*A Devotional Anthology for the Dioskouroi and Their Families*

Sirius Rising:
>*A Devotional Anthology for Cynocephalic Deities*